THE NAVY OF HUMANKIND: WASP SQUADRON

BOOK

ACE

Colonel Jonathan P. Brazee
USMC (Ret)

A Semper Fi Press Book

ISBN-13: 978-1-945743-30-6
ISBN-10: 1-945743-30-1   (Semper Fi Press)

Printed in the United States of America

Acknowledgements:

I want to thank all those who took the time to offer advice as I wrote his book. A special shout-out goes to real Navy air warrior, CAPT imothy "Spike" Prendergast, USN (Ret.) for keeping helping me th "air-speak" and culture, and to my beta readers James Caplan, lly O'Donnell, Micky Cocker, and Jim McNeill for their valuable ut.

Cover by Jude Beers

DEDICATION

Captain Kimberly Nicole Hampton, U.S. Army
OH-58D Pilot
Shot down and KIA 2 January 2004
Fallujah, Iraq

AUTHOR'S NOTE

The events taking place in Chapter 12 were originally described in "The Pumpkin Ace," a short story published in *Bob's Bar 2*, published by LMBPN Publishing.

The original short story was set in a bar where the characters were relating sea stories to each other. In *Ace*, the story has been modified in both content and style to fit this book.

SG-62998

Chapter 1

"Standby. Launch in five . . . four . . ."

Unable to pull out the silver cross that hung around her neck from under her flight suit, Petty Officer Second Class Floribeth Salinas O'Shea Dalisay, Navy of Humankind, mimed the act, touching her chest, then raising her hand and kissing her empty fingers.

". . . three . . . two . . . one . . . launch."

She returned Josh's salute as he stood with the others on the observation deck before the *Tala II* was shot down the launch rail out into the black, leaving the vast bulk of the *DS Victory* behind.

Beth kept her eyes on her display—not that she could do much if something went wrong except wait for a pickup. Flight ops aboard a carrier were hectic, almost panic-filled evolutions. *Victory's* huge size was only relative, and there were too many moving parts in too little space to rely on human pilots. Everything was automated out of Primary Flight Control (PryFly), to include her powerful FC engine kicking on. She was just a passenger for the time being.

Her display was an explosion of multi-colored traces as the ten flights of fighters spread out on slightly diverging paths—a collision at these speeds would ruin anyone's day.

"You hanging in there?" Mercy asked over the S2S.

"Just waiting for the release of control," she told her wingman and best friend. "I hate this part of it."

"Don't get your panties in a twist, sista. We'll be getting action soon enough."

"I don't wear panties in my flight suit," Beth grumbled without keying the transmitter. Too hard to hook up the flightsuit's plumbing attachments with anything between the suit and her bare skin.

But Mercy was right. If there were FALs in the system, they'd be in a fight soon enough. She wasn't doing herself any favors getting worked up. She needed to be at her mental and physical best when . . . if . . . it came to a fight.

Being part—a very small part—of Task Force Iron Shield, the first Navy task force to go on the offensive against the crystals, was emotionally rewarding, but life aboard the ship was much different than that on Sierra Station. Commander Tuominen, their CO, had been in control during their commissioning and work-ups, for all practical purposes. Now, he was small fry among the task force's admirals and captains.

That made the mere fighter pilots almost inconsequential.

But it's up to us to take it to the FALs, she told herself as she waited for the release.

At point-nine kiloklicks, far, far beyond the point where her engine exhaust could wear and tear the carrier, control was returned to her.

"Kick some ass, Stingers," Flight Control passed on the squadron net.

"Thanks for the lift, Fox-Charlie," the commander passed before giving the command to synch check and arm their weapons.

The *Tala* was purring like a kitten, all readouts green, but Beth dutifully told Rose, her AI, to run the check. As expected, everything was in fine order. Not that she expected anything less. Even with the continual mods made by Jean-Luc's team, Josh was able to keep the *Tala* in top shape.

"Arm weapons," she ordered her AI, then watched as each of the four LEDs clicked to green.

Three of her weapons systems—the L-40 Laser, the P13B Hadron Beamer, and the G-21 Railgun were the same as on her last mission, but her M-57X torpedo was a new, test version of the normal M-57, something cooked up by Jean

Luc and his team based on the analysis of the crystal ship Beth and Mercy had captured on Toowoomba. The *Tala* was one of two Wasps with the test version, and Beth was itching to give it a go.

"Helmets on," he ordered as Beth suppressed a groan. The new PP-42's, referred to as "neck-crackers," were the latest and greatest from Jean Luc's's R&D labs. The science-types still weren't exactly sure how the FALs' energy weapons worked, but they could analyze the effects of the beams. They destroyed not only electronics, but also nervous systems. The new helmets were designed to create canceling fields, theoretically protecting the wearers' brains.

The pilots hated them for two reasons. First, they each massed 4.7 kg, and wearing them was exhausting, hence the "neck-cracker" moniker. Second, unlike their old helmets, there was no face shield. A face shield evidently could not generate the counteracting web. Without a face shield, they could not see out of them. Each helmet had to be hardwired into a jack newly installed into each Wasp, and all of the images were then fed into the display film inside each one.

Jean Luc swore that there was no practical difference from the nano-tube channels that had previously allowed the pilots to see through the integral canopies, and that in some ways, this was even better. To a person, however, each of the pilots felt that the helmets distanced themselves from the action. A good pilot became one with their Wasp, and this didn't help.

Beth twisted her neck a few times, connected the hardwire, slipped the heavy helmet on, and then ran her checks.

"Form up," the commander passed as the last Wasp confirmed readiness. "And let's see if we can jump some FALs."

"Did he just say 'FALs?' As in 'Fucking Aliens?'" Mercy asked excitedly.

"That's what he said," Beth answered.

She understood Mercy's surprise—and joy. Mercy had a mouth that would make a wet-water navy sailor blush, but the commander, like most of the Golden Tribe, was far more circumspect. He tended to use the officially designated NSB-1's (for Nonhuman Sentient Being-Ones) with possibly a few references of "crystals." But "FALs?" For "Fucking Alien Lifeforms?" The commander must be getting contaminated with his constant contact with norms.

She didn't have time to wonder how else their commander had sunk to join the dark side. They had launched in a spread pattern. Now, they had to maneuver into their assault formation as they advanced on where the vast military AIs back on Earth and Chariter had given a 74% probability of crystal activity. Ten flights were in the force—four were arrayed in a diamond to provide security, while six were leading the assault itself. Twenty-four Wasp FX6-Kilos. The finest fighters built by humankind . . .

. . . potentially facing an untold number of crystals. With the new mods Jean-Luc and his crew had developed, a single Wasp should be the match of any single crystal ship. *Should* being the operative word here. The crystals had not remained static since first contact, either, and for all Beth knew, if there were FALs up ahead, they could be the latest and greatest the crystalline chlorine-breathers could produce.

It would be nice to have one of the task force's destroyers along with them. Heck, even one of the task force's two monitors. But the monitors weren't fast enough to keep up, and the powers-that-be didn't want to risk one of the ultraexpensive capital ships until more was understood about the crystals' capabilities.

In the great European land battles of the 17th and 18th Centuries, ground troops were used as "cannon fodder," advancing until they started taking fire, thereby revealing to their commanders the range of the enemy artillery. Beth thought she now knew how those long-dead soldiers felt.

So, as in each of the previous engagements, it was to be the single-seat Wasps to take it to the enemy. VFX-99, the Stingers, had already been blooded, and along with their newlycommissioned sister squadron, VFX-21, the Scorpions, they would continue to be the point of the spear until all of the Navy's ships had been upgraded.

Which put them into harm's way more often than not while the rest of the Navy played spectator.

Not that Beth minded. She *wanted* to mix it up with the FALs—she had lost friends to the hunks of animated crystal, and she needed payback.

Hyped-up passing through the gate, adrenaline coursing through her veins, the reality of interstellar war reared its head, however. Unlike the holovids of ships dogfighting at close range, real fighting took place at long distances. And with the task force exiting the new gate outside the SG-62998 system, it was going to take some time to approach.

Mercy was right. Real or imaginary, she couldn't let her panties get in a twist.

Beth took four deep breaths, then pulled down the drink nipple on her dispenser, flipping the sixth selector, and took a long swallow, a smile cracking her face as cold heaven slid down her throat. Completely against Navy regulations, her trusty plane captain had managed, once again, to slip Coke into the canteen. The other five would have the required hot and cold boosters, full of the nutrients and boosters guaranteed to maximize performance, but for Beth, nothing worked like a Coke to clear the mind.

She took another swallow, let out a belch that would make Mercy proud, and settled in to wait.

****

"I'm going to splash me one," Mercy passed less than three hours later as Fox Flight pursued two crystal ships of the eleven that had scattered like a covey of quail.

One moment, the sensors were showing anomalies, the next moment, every display was lit up like a Christmas tree as the crystal ships shot out from the vicinity of Planet #4.

"That's a negative, Red Devil," Gollum passed. "Priority goes to Fire Ant. We need to see if the 57X is going to have effect on target."

"There's two of them," Mercy muttered, but on the S2S with Beth and not on the flight net.

Beth knew that Mercy ached for a kill, and despite their being best friends above and beyond being wingmates, she was jealous of Beth's own three kills. Not that she'd ever said anything, but Beth could sense it.

Beth could empathize with her, but that didn't mean she wanted to give up another shot of her own. With three kills to her credit, she had more than any other living pilot, and with two more, she'd become the first Navy Ace in 200 years. She felt a little bad about that, not wanting to give up a chance of a kill so Mercy could finally flame a FAL, but it wasn't her fault that she'd been given the 57X. The R&D types wanted to see if this version of the torpedo would be more effective, and so the admiral herself had told the commander to assign them to Beth and Wingnut, a CWO4 in Delta Flight with two kills under his belt.

"That's right. There's two of them," Beth said, feeling guilty knowing that she'd splash both if she could. She didn't have to tell Mercy that, however.

Not that she was sure anyone would get a kill. Unlike on previous missions, the crystals were not attacking but rather running instead. The eggheads still were not sure exactly how the crystal ships jumped, but they seemed to be able to do it independently, not like human ships that had to go through a gate. Two of the Wasps in Mike Flight were towing some sophisticated arrays that would record and upload data if the crystals jumped so the scientists could try and figure that out.

The human fighters had the advantage of speed at the moment and were closing, but Beth kept expecting to see the fighters wink out before Fox and Golf were within range.

In ship-to-ship combat, where both were trying to splash the other, a speed advantage was not that relevant. The two enemy fighters, labeled "A" and "B" on the display, would be closing with the Wasps at the same rate as the Wasps were closing with them. But when one was trying to run, the faster ship, whether the one running or the one chasing, had the advantage.

She glanced over at the other flights, now released from central control and chasing assigned targets. Unless the FALs turned to fight, she wasn't sure there would be any engagement. "Gollum, should we goose them with the Forties?" Capgun asked on the Fox Flight net.

"No. Let's not give them anything to make them jump sooner," the lieutenant commander answered.

Beth was not surprised. First, that the Fox Flight leader said no, and second, that Capgun had asked. While the lasers might have what was essentially unlimited range, they had not proven effective against the crystal ships and had fallen out of favor. Capgun, with two kills flying the *Lovely Rita*, though, would also like to add to his tally. While not as overtly anxious as Mercy, Beth knew he wanted in on the fight just as much as her friend did.

Heck, for all she knew, since these FALs were running, they might be the crystal equivalent of civilian ships and possibly be vulnerable to the lasers. She wasn't going to bring that up, however. No use giving the lieutenant any ideas.

Her eyes drifted to the bottom of the *Tala's* display being projected onto the inside of her neck-cracker. Her three torps, two of the X's and one normal 57, were in the launcher, still green and ready to go. The Wasp had a haptic HUD, adjusted to the pilot's preferences. Beth liked a clean display, so she had the routine readouts on the opaque area below the projected canopy display

I just hope I get to use you guys.

Beth kept refreshing her display, hoping that the linked AIs were forming a better picture of what they faced. She started running firing solutions, not that she was in effective range yet. Through the wizardry of quantum fold mechanics, something that was basically magic to her for all intents and purposes, she had the general location of the crystal ships, but Beth liked to have the more specific data that her scanners would gather as the range closed. The more she could input into the torps, the better the chance of a kill. At this range, it would still take her torps 25 minutes to reach the FALs, and that was if they cooperated by keeping their ships on their current course and rate of acceleration.

From Beth's experiences so far, she didn't think the FALs were likely to cooperate.

The next 45 minutes was a slow-motion chase . . . all happening at .72C. The lieutenant used the four Wasps of Fox Flight to herd the two crystal ships where their fighters would be in position for mutual supporting fires. Beth might have the first shot, but if she missed, the lieutenant would unleash the other three fighters.

Slowly developing battles were nothing new for navies. Beth had just read an account of the First Barbary War back on Earth during the early 19th Century. In the days of sail, ships might maneuver for hours, or even days, all for a momentary pass where they could train their guns on the enemy ship. A smaller ship with fewer guns could sink a much better-armed foe by winning the maneuver battle.

In this particular fight, the *Tala* was the better-armed ship. She hoped. She couldn't allow the FAL to outmaneuver her. She expanded out her display to take in the entire operation. Each four-Wasp flight had broken off from the others to pursue one or two FALs. That made Beth a little uncomfortable. They were unable to support each other if this was all part of the enemy plan, to divide and conquer. She didn't see any evidence of crystal ships lying in wait, ready for an ambush, but then again, it wouldn't be much of an ambush if they were evident. The FALs had ambushed Navy fighters before, after all.

Beth asked her AI to run a probability that this was an ambush, but there wasn't enough data for any meaningful result.

"Are they leading us away from the other flights on purpose?" she asked Mercy. "Separating us from our mutual support?"

"No. They're just running like scared little . . . oh, shit. That's a good point," Mercy said. "Think they are?"

"Don't know. Just too much time thinking. Over thinking, probably."

"What does Gollum think?" Mercy asked.

"I didn't ask him," she said, wondering if she should bring it up, then deciding against it. The Fox Flight leader was an experienced pilot, and she was still a relative newbie.

Still, she diverted another 10% of her systems to scan for any sign of an ambush. Better safe than sorry, and she was still slaving into the flight web with the other three fighters. It wasn't as if she was blinding herself to the two FALs they were chasing.

As if on cue, the two FALs split and diverged. The Wasps had been slowly closing the gap, and the crystals must have figured they couldn't jump from the system before the humans were within range.

"Fire Ant, on me. Capgun and Red Devil, take the Bravo target. Let's splash them!"

"Take the trail," he passed to Beth on the S2S.

For a moment, Beth wondered if he was going for the kill himself forgetting that she had the mission priority.

"Let's see if I can get his attention while you test the Xray," he passed.

She let him pull ahead, keeping "below" him on the galactic plane. What he said made sense. He could start hammering at the FAL with his P-13, battering at the FAL's shielding and commanding its attention while Beth set up the shot with her torp.

"Kick some ass," Mercy passed as she and Capgun broke off.

If this was a set-up, the FALs had just broken them up even further. She took a quick glance at the overall mission. It was messy, a melee, without any evidence of the teamwork that made the Directorate Navy so effective. It made her uncomfortable, but she couldn't see any direct threat forming that would indicate they were being played.

Don't worry about them, Floribeth. You just need to focus on the FAL in front of you.

"Let's see if I can tingle its ass," Gollum passed. A moment later, he fired his P-13, the hadron beam cannon. While the beam traveled almost at the speed of light, it would still take almost 20 seconds to reach the crystal ship. The FAL, however, almost reacted immediately, juking to the right abruptly. A split second later, the FAL fired back.

That revealed two things. First, the ship was, in fact, a fighter, not some FAL version of a freighter or vacation liner. Second, it confirmed that the crystals had either quantum scanners or some equivalent to detect weapons fire before the beam actually arrived on target.

The Fox Flight leader didn't bother to maneuver as he poured fire at the FAL, chasing it as it looped tightly back, but still covering kiloklicks as it turned to fight. No manned human ship could withstand that amount of force. A Wasp making the same maneuver would probably be beyond the fighter's compensators to keep from turning the pilot into so much jelly. The Wasps seemed to have the speed advantage, but the FALs had proven themselves to be more maneuverable, the FAL's crystalline bodies biologically better suited to G-forces.

Beth let the *Tala* drift off of Gollum's flank as he and the FAL exchanged fire. The *Jenny's* shields were degrading under the fire, but the flight leader kept her steady, pouring more and more gigajoules out of his cannon and onto the FAL.

"Hope your nect-cracker works," she muttered to herself, worried about the punishment Gollum was absorbing.

Beth kept running firing solutions, watching the POS, the Probability of Success, climb as they both closed.

"Any time now, Fire Ant," Gollum passed as the *Jenny's* shielding reached 50%.

Beth was still at a 52% POS, but she had to act. She fired the first M-57X, then pushed the *Tala* to the max in a tight turn, the heavy G's pushing the compensators to their limits, which made her nerves crawl as if her body was being invaded by tiny ants. She hated the feeling, but the excitement of battle overtook the discomfort.

She waited ten seconds before firing the second torpedo, giving it a slightly different aspect and hopefully diverting the FAL's attention even more. Now it was up to Jean Luc's new babies.

Not that Beth was simply going to watch. The FAL was still firing on the flight leader, and the *Jenny's* shielding was down to 43%. Beth targeted her own P-13 on the crystal ship and fired, hoping to draw the enemy fire away from Gollum.

Within moments, the FAL's fire shifted from him, but not to the *Tala*. The crystal ship evidently detected the M-57Xs and took them under fire. This was the real test. Could they stand up to the intense beam weapon and get a hit on the enemy ship? With 112 "regular" M-57s fired on FALs so far, only 13 had hit their targets, with 11 kills.

Beth barely noticed when the lieutenant commander fired one of his M-57s as an insurance policy. She kept up her P-13 fire, but her attention was focused on her two Xs. She yelled out in frustration when the first detonated still 18 kiloklicks from the target. One of the changes in the X version was that instead of simply breaking apart or going inert, the torpedo had an internal "dead-man's switch." If power failed, it would detonate. But at 18 kiloclicks, the FAL was too far away to be affected.

Twelve seconds later, however, the second X hit home, blowing the FAL into its component atoms.

"Damn right!" Beth yelled, the thrill of victory taking over her.

"Nice shooting," Gollum said. "Now let's get over and help Capgun."

Crap. Forgot about them, she thought guiltily.

Beth pulled up the Combat Awareness display. Mercy and Capgun had flanked the crystal ship and were pouring fire into it. Beth had watched a documentary filmed on one of the vast wildlife refuges back on Earth, where two lions were trying to bring down a cape buffalo, darting in and out as the beast kept them at bay, blood pouring down his black hide from various gashes and bites. The fight ahead reminding her of that scene as she and the lieutenant commander rushed to support the other two.

Beth checked the Battle Diary. Mercy had already fired two torpedoes. Neither had hit, but both she and Capgun had been hitting the ship with their beam cannons, and the combined fire was having an effect. The crystal ship's shields had to be degrading. Despite the distance, Gollum and Beth fired as well, adding more gigajoules that pounded on the enemy ship.

The FAL was getting hit on all sides, but it still had a bite of its own. It fired two torpedoes, one heading for Mercy, the other, oddly enough, Beth thought, heading for her and Gollum, ignoring Capgun. And like a cape buffalo trying to break free by charging one of the lions, the FAL changed course to head right at Mercy.

And it almost worked. Mercy had to shift her beam cannon fire to the torpedo targeting her, as did Beth and Gollum. The crystal torps did not seem as effective as the humans', but they were more than enough to destroy a Wasp if it detonated close. However, by pushing its quick attack on Mercy, Gollum, and Beth, it left Capgun uncovered. The chief warrant officer fired two M-57s.

At 200 kiloklicks range, it took his torps only five seconds to reach the crystal ship. The first one destroyed the FAL, just as her combined fire with Gollum destroyed the torp honing in on them.

Beth immediately shifted her targeting to the torpedo closing in on Mercy, but unnecessarily. It detonated a couple of kiloklicks away from her friend. Close enough for a serious pucker factor, but not dangerous.

Beth felt a twinge of disappointment that Capgun had gotten the FAL kill. She'd already splashed one of the crystals, but she had wanted both.

Are there any more? she wondered, expanding her display to include the entire mission force.

Yes, there were more FALs. Of the 12 crystal ships insystem, only three had been splashed: hers, Capgun's, and Wingnut had gotten one with his 57X. No Wasp had been lost, but Teabag from Bravo Flight had his Wasp damaged and was being escorted back to the gate.

"What now?" Capgun asked on the flight net, his voice high with excitement.

"Wait a sec," the lieutenant commander said, then, "Let's see if we can support Kilo."

Looking at her display, Beth agreed that was the most logical course of action. Not that she thought it would do any good. The four Wasps in Kilo Flight were closing in on a single FAL, and they'd splash the sucker long before Fox Flight or Golf could get in range.

Something bothered her about the Battle Area of Operations, but she couldn't quite place it. There were 21 Wasps still in the fight, facing nine FALs. They had an overwhelming numbers advantage.

"Should we G-Shot it?" Mercy asked on the flight net, her voice eager with anticipation.

"No!" Beth shouted, not waiting for the flight leader to answer. She'd G-Shotted before, letting the chemicals invade her body to allow her to survive Gs the *Tala's* compensators couldn't handle. And she'd gone through the two-week recovery from that as well.

"That's a negative," Gollum passed. "We'll let Kilo handle it for now."

"Then why are we rushing halfway across this system?" Mercy asked Beth on the S2S.

Beth didn't answer.

For the next five minutes, she watched the slow-motion ballet play out, her display weaving lines depicting human and FAL ships' traces. It was kind of pretty, if one could forget that they represented life and death struggles.

Three of three of the groupings branched out and away from each other before two started to come back . . .

"That's it!" Beth shouted into her mic just as the battle AI issued a warning, the red glow covering her helmet display.

If the tracks of the three groupings were projected forward, then six FALs would converge on Bravo, giving them a short, but real, six-on-four advantage. Alpha and Delta would eventually arrive to reverse the advantage, but could Bravo hold out?

The commander was evidently not confident that they could. Within seconds after the AI's warning, he ordered Bravo to break contact and hook up with Alpha. They would still pursue, but as an eight-Wasp flight. He was not going to let the nine crystal ships isolate any Wasps where they could gain a numerical advantage.

"They shot their load with that," Mercy said on the S2S. "Are they going to bug out now?"

"Don't know," Beth said.

She thought they would, though. They were still outnumbered, after all. The question was how much farther was the commander going to chase them. Every kiloklick separated the flights more and more.

The commander must have been on the same wavelength as she was. He ordered Delta to join Alpha and Bravo and Fox to join up with Golf and Echo. With twelve Wasps in one section and nine in the other, they were to abandon pursuit of five of the remaining FALs and just focus on four of them.

Beth felt better about not being so dispersed, but she kept waiting for the other shoe to drop.

Which it did sixteen minutes later. It must have become evident to the FALs that the humans were not going to be led on a goose-chase and get separated from each other because oneafter-the-other, more crystal ships started popping into the system. Two, four, eight, twelve, sixteen. Within a minute, it was the humans who were outnumbered.

Beth felt her warrior surge within her. She'd felt uncomfortable, even nervous before. Her sixth sense had told her something was up, but she couldn't figure it out. But now that the FALs had played their hand, she knew what she faced, and she wanted to engage. She checked her weapons status. No torpedoes left, but she didn't need them to splash crystals.

"Bravo-Charlie, Bravo-Charlie," the commander ordered as his command was also splashed across her helmet display.

"No!" she objected, but to herself, not over the net.

"Bravo-Charlie" was the order to break contact, to return to the gate.

"Condition Blue," he added.

Which meant, if it was needed, to G-Shot.

Beth wasn't happy, but the rational side of her realized that he was right. They were now outnumbered, and there could be more FALs ready to make an appearance. Their primary mission was to test the M-57Xs, and that had been done. There wasn't a pressing reason to risk the squadron.

It more than a little burned her craw to be abandoning the field of battle when things had seemed so well in hand, but she knew the commander was right. He had to decide what was best for the squadron, and with their primary mission accomplished, getting back in one piece trumped another battle.

It still sucks, though, she thought as she pulled the *Tala* around for the dash to the gate.

FS VICTORY

Chapter 2

The tractors took hold, bringing the *Tala* into the hangar and gently onto the landing pad. Beth stayed in the cockpit as the yellowshirts, running around in organized chaos, raced to the eight Wasps. A yellowshirt gave her a thumbs up, then connected the lift mule. The *Tala* jerked upwards before he shifted the mule into forward and pulled the fighter out of the way so the next eight could land.

Admiral Nzama and Commodore LaRue stood silently as Fox and Golf were taxied to their pads, but Beth could feel their gaze burn into them. The mission had not been completely successful, but both Wingnut and she had fired their 57X's and splashed their targets. Capgun had splashed one as well. The primary mission had been completed, even if it had been a little ugly, with one Wasp damaged and then ceding the field of battle in the end.

Josh was waiting impatiently as the *Tala* was nudged into position, then settled onto the hangar deck, eager to check out his baby. No one could move, however, until the line commander gave the OK. Finally, he signaled that all eight Wasps were in position and secured, and Beth popped the canopy. Before she was halfway out of the cockpit, Josh had pushed up the small ladder for her and was running his checks.

"In case you were wondering, I'm fine," she said, as facing the fighter, she reached down blindly with her foot, stretching until her toe hit the top of the ladder. She'd taken a lot of razzing for using the step ladder at first, but her combat record quickly quelled that.

"I know you are," Josh said, not looking around as he ran his scanmaster over the sensor array in the *Tala's* nose. "I need to know if the *Tala* is."

She shook her head affectionately and hopped down to the deck.

"I knew you couldn't let me catch up to you," Capgun said, coming over to slap her on the back. "You just had to get one more."

"That sort of was the whole intent of the mission, right? I mean, Wingnut and me."

"Yeah, but new tech, you know? Using that advantage to keep the crown? Hardly sporting, if you ask me," he said with a laugh.

"And you two could have left something for the rest of us," Mercy said, joining them. "Spread the wealth, you know."

Mercy's voice was light, and she was smiling, but Beth knew lacking even one kill was heavy on her psyche. It wasn't as if it was Beth's fault, though. She didn't write the orders.

She wanted to reassure her friend, to tell her she'd get a kill in time, but she didn't know if it was true. The FALs might get Mercy first. They might get Capgun or her before they could rack up another kill, for that matter. But more than that, she knew Mercy's pride would take that as pandering.

The next group of Wasps was already settling into position. Even after almost two years, Beth still was impressed by the choreography of the deck crew, getting the squadron aboard so quickly and in such a confined space. Commander Tuominen was among this group. He popped his canopy and started to extricate himself, all arms and legs like a spider coming out of a hole. The GT was too tall to be a Wasp pilot, and Beth didn't know how he could jam his long body into the cockpit.

"I wouldn't want to be in his shoes," Mercy said, tilting her head to indicate the admiral and commodore. "They look pretty pissed."

"Pissed? Why? We kicked butt," Capgun said, still on a high after splashing another FAL.

"No, we didn't. And we had to run away."

Capgun's eyebrows furrowed, his mouth opened, but whatever he was about to say was cut off.

"Capgun, Fire Ant, you're wanted in eighty-six," Lieutenant Ramsey-Chord shouted over to them from where he was standing by Redeye's *Georgie* with AT1 Luvkin, the plane captain.

"Eighty-six? For the debrief?" Capgun asked.

"I'm just passing the word," the maintenance officer said, pointing to his earbud.

"Me, too?" Mercy asked.

"Just those two," the lieutenant said, before he hurried down the line, shouting at another of the plane captains.

Debriefs were conducted in one of the secured spaces near the CIC, guarded by an armed Marine who took retinal scans before allowing anyone entry. Even the admiral had to relent to the scans.

"Eighty-six" was C-1-8-6, the wardroom in Non-Sec Country, the small island in the middle of the ship where civilians and others without full clearance were berthed while underway. Beth had been in the space once before, when a visiting Directorate bigwig had come aboard and given the pilots what he obviously thought was a pep talk. Most of the ship's crew avoided "Nonsense" Country like the plague, leaving that to the ship's public affairs staff.

A lieutenant commander met them at the hatch. Beth recognized her from the daily "State of the Ship" broadcasts each morning as the ship's Public Affairs officer.

"Sorry for the short notice," the lieutenant commander said. "We've got the press assembled inside, and we've been ordered to make you available to them.

Capgun nudged Beth with his elbow. He'd told her that with the Navy wanting to garner public support, they'd soon be focusing on the fighters with the most kills, giving faces to the war effort. She'd thought he was crazy, but evidently, he'd been right.

"I wouldn't have done it this way, but this comes from way up the chain," the officer continued, more to herself than to the two of them. "But it is what it is, and we'll cope, like always.

"First, anything operational is off-limits. You can talk about yourself, how you feel, and things like that, but nothing about the mission, your ships, or the crystals. Do not offer your opinions on what you think they are or what they want, understand?"

Both pilots nodded.

"I'll be in there with you, and I'll intercede if things go astray, so don't get stressed. Just relax and be yourselves. Oh, and be positive, OK?"

They both nodded again.

"This isn't going to be the last time, so, I'll be giving you classes starting tomorrow on how to handle yourselves. All of you pilots. But for now, just smile and do your best."

She gave each a clap on the shoulder, then opened the hatch, ushering the two inside.

"How does it feel be one kill away from making ace, Petty Officer Dalisay?" a young man shouted out at they entered the space.

"You'll have time for questions after the brief, Hyatt," the PA officer said

Eight civilians were gathered in the room, all with predatory looks on their faces, almost salivating at the sight of the fighter pilots. Beth swallowed, pulled out her crucifix and kissed it before slipping it back under her flightsuit.

Beth was relieved to see Wingnut, the commander, Captain Restov (the ship's XO), and a master chief she didn't recognize, in the space as well. At least the three pilots were not being thrown to the wolves alone. And they *were* wolves, on the hunt for food to feed the masses.

Captain Restov nodded as the two arrived, waving a hand for them to join Wingnut, before he addressed the civilians. "Now, back from their mission, we have Chief Warrant Officer Four Wylie Pashton, Warrant Officer James Caplan, and Petty Officer Floribeth Dalisay. As previously briefed, all three splashed NSB-1 fighters, and with three, three, and four kills respectively, they are the Navy's current tally leaders.

"Remember, the actual mission itself is off limits. I'm sure you can understand why."

"We're not crystals," one of the press muttered, something the XO ignored.

"So, without further ado, here are our fighters," he said, waving a hand in a sweep toward them as he stepped back. "How does it feel be just a single kill away from making ace, Petty Officer Dalisay?" the young reporter—Hyatt, the PA had called him—yelled out, beating the others to the punch.

How do I feel? What a weird question. How am I supposed to answer that?

She looked up, not to the PA, but to Commander Tuominen. He gave her the slightest of nods in encouragement.

Am I supposed to be humble? Boldly assertive? She wished the PA had already given them whatever classes they needed to handle the press.

"I . . . this isn't about me," she said. "I'm just one pilot in the Stingers, and whatever success we have had is a result of the training we've received and the combined effort of all of us, from pilots to maintenance teams to the entire ship's crew. I may have fired the tor . . . shots that downed the crystals," she said, changing "torpedo" to "shot," keeping in mind the PA's orders to stay away from specifics.

She looked back up to the commander, and he nodded again, this time in approval.

"That's all well and good, Petty Officer Dalisay," another reporter said, mispronouncing her name as "DAL-is-ee." "But you were the one who's killed four of the enemy, not the entire ship's crew. So, how do you feel about that?"

"Proud," she said, her inflection rising at the end of the word as if in a question. "I mean, this is what we've been trained to do, and I'm proud that I've been given the opportunity."

"VFX-99 and VFX-21 have had their Wasps modified, something that other ships are being—"

"Rynona, I'm afraid that's getting into the technical aspects," the PAO interrupted.

"I wasn't going there," the bald woman said. "I just wanted to know if the retrofits—whatever they are—will benefit our capital ships, which you know are property of the citizenship, expensive property at that."

"No, Rynona, just no. No one is going to answer that. Anyone else?"

"It says here," an older man said, looking at his tab and addressing Beth, "that you used to be a commercial exploratory pilot with Hamdani Brothers. That's something quite different than being a Navy fighter pilot, I'm guessing. What's the biggest difference?"

This one's easy.

"I was always on my own in my Hummingbird. Here, I'm out there with the best pilots in the galaxy," she said, pointing at Capgun and Wingnut. "I'm never on my own."

"And I couldn't ask for a better wingman than Fire Ant," Capgun interrupted, to Beth's relief. "She's a fine pilot, one of the best . . . but I'll beat both her and Wingnut to ace."

That brought a laugh and shifted the focus from Beth. Capgun was a natural, an easy speaker with enough bravado and humor to keep the reporters' attention. Beth and Wingnut barely had to speak. It wasn't that Beth was shy. She had a healthy ego, as most fighter jocks did, but she wasn't sure what the Navy wanted her to say, and Captain Rostov's presence was a reminder that the brass had their own agenda. She was more than willing to let Capgun take the spotlight and risk saying the wrong thing.

Captain Restov cut the presser short after five more minutes, citing the operational brief that was about to start that required the three pilots' and Commander Tuominen's participation.

Beth was grateful to get out of there intact. She was a fighter pilot, not a public affairs sailor. But from the reporters' attention, she realized that she and the others were of high interest to the public. They were the face of the war so far.

She knew there would be more pressers, more interviews. But not until she'd gone through whatever training the PAO and
her staff had for them . . . she hoped.

Chapter 3

"Lick my toes, Hyatt," Beth ordered the reporter to the howls of laughter of her court.

"Yes, Queen Neptune," the reporter said, and still on his knees, crawled up to her, bent over, and licked the squishy and vile-smelling concoction Chief Weiscamp—otherwise known as the Royal Consort—had squirted on them from a plastic squeeze bottle.

The reporter had demanded to be able to attend the Crossing the Line ceremony and report on it, stating that it would be good PR.   The admiral had agreed . . . but as pollywog.   He had to participate.   Of course, as Queen Neptune, it was up to Beth, and she'd happily agreed.

Beth had been surprised that out of the entire ship, she was the senior shellback. Almost all of the Hamdani Brothers Exploratory Corps had crossed the Tanis Line, the imaginary boundary between the inner and outer Orion Arm, at one point or another. It was considered no big deal, and there wasn't a ceremony marking it. The Navy, however, hewed to traditions millennia old, and the Crossing the Line ceremony, rarely celebrated, was one of the most cherished.

Navy scouts and packets often ventured inward on the Orion Arm, but on the *Victory*, only 22 sailors and one Marine had crossed the line, and none before a 19-year-old Beth had crossed it eight years before. That made her the senior shellback and Queen Neptune for the ceremony.

Not that the ship was exactly at the Tanis Line, but after the last gate jump, the task force had entered the inner spiral. Four of the six ships were now conducting their ceremonies, and the remaining two would as soon as they were relieved from picket duty.

The reporter dug in, forcing his tongue between her toes, which felt decidedly weird. She had to resist jerking back. "Arise, Pollywog Hyatt," she said cutting off his efforts, which he seemed to be enjoying entirely too much. "Take your royal bath."

In the early days of sail, the "royal bath" might mean a dunking in the southern seas. Vacuum not being conducive to human life, aboard the *Victory*, the royal bath was a line of six large pots full of briny water. The next bath up had to be continually topped off due to the eager ministrations of Lieutenant Wehm, one of her Bath Attendants.

Hyatt gave her a wink as he leaned back, then knee-crawled over to Wehm and the bath.

"Cleanse ye of your pollywog slime," the lieutenant roared, his voice still going strong after almost two thousand pollywogs.

He grabbed Hyatt around the back of his neck and forced the reporter's head into the brine, shaking it around for good measure and splashing a good amount onto the deck. Beth was surprised all of the spillages hadn't eaten through the deck like sulphuric acid, so strong it was. The deck might stand up to it, but not so human eyes. Most of the new shellbacks had eyes as red as the demons of hell.

She didn't have time to watch the reporter. With about 2000 sailors and Marines, they had to keep the line moving.

"Pollywog Tuominen," Sergeant Lancelot Watson, a hulking Marine and her Royal Baby announced.

Most of the pollywogs simply marched up, kissed her grease-covered belly, and then moved on to get their bath, the final event before becoming shellbacks. Certain notable people, however, deserved more attention, and her CO was one of them.

She suddenly felt self-conscious, in her crown, green halter, and scaled green skirt, split up the middle. She'd gotten used to the line of men and woman giving her belly a peck. It had been awkward at first. More than awkward. When she pulled up the traditions of the ceremony, she'd seen images of large, potbellied chiefs as King Neptune, presenting their bellies to be kissed by the polliwogs in subservience. Beth, however, was petite, and her belly was tiny. It was a small target. She was sitting on a throne, but the polliwogs still had to kneel between her legs and lean in to kiss her. After every ten or twenty polliwogs, the chief had to reapply more slime to her belly with the squirt bottle he kept in a jury-rigged holster hanging from his beefy shoulder.

Awkward at first, it had quickly become a routine, an assembly line. This was her CO, though, a member of the Golden Tribe. Among the remaining 20 or so polliwogs were the ship's senior officers and the admiral herself. She had delighted in giving Mercy, Capgun, even Gollum, her flight leader, more attention, but this was different.

No, it's not. Look at him. He expects something, she realized, pushing aside her initial intention to just have him give her a quick kiss on the belly and move on.

"Dance," she ordered.

"Excuse me?" the commander asked, confused.

"'Excuse me Queen Neptune,' don't you mean?"

"Uh, yes. Of course. Excuse me Queen Neptune?"

"Did I stutter? I ordered you to dance. A jig. And make it good," she ordered as those within hearing broke out into laughter and shouted catcalls.

He stepped back, looked around, then broke into a halting dance, his arms rising above his head as his long legs gracefully pranced. Whether it was a jig or not, Beth didn't know. She really had no idea what a jig was, only that it was nautical.

"Spin around," she ordered.

Damn, he's good, she thought as he twirled.

Like all of the polliwogs, his uniform was inside out, and he still dripped from crawling through the "Hog Trough," a chute filled with nasty things the chief had gathered. Yet even so, he was impressive, almost noble. The GTs had that effect on norms. That was one reason they'd risen in power over the centuries.

"Halt, Polliwog Tuominen," she said. "You're boring me."

He spun gracefully to a stop, unable to keep the tiniest of smiles from turning up the corner of his mouth.

"You may now kiss the royal belly."

Even kneeling and with her on a throne, his head was well above hers, and he had to bend low between her legs to kiss her. She felt a tingle of . . . she didn't want to know of what or even think about it. He was her CO, and a GT to boot. She grabbed him by the ears as he kissed her and pushed him up. She'd smushed Mercy's face into her belly, rubbing it deep into the slime, but that wasn't going to happen with him.

"Arise, Polliwog Tuominen," she said, her voice cracking ever-so-slightly. "Take your royal bath."

"Yes, my queen," the commander said before turning to the next tub in line. Lieutenant Wehm seemed disappointed that he didn't get the commander.

More of the crew, old shellbacks and new shellbacks alike, crowded closer as the final officers performed their penance. Beth tried to make it good, and from the responses, she thought she'd succeeded. The admiral was last, and Beth put her through the most, first having her sing the ship's song, then the Anthem of Man, all perched on one leg. She had to get on her hands and knees and bark like a seal, clapping her hands like flippers, before Beth allowed her to kiss her belly.

Wehm was next up for the bath, but he was a little more subdued with the admiral, just dunking her head and letting her back up, to the catcalls of the observers. Big, bad Lieutenant Wehm just blushed and pointed to where the Royal Scribe handed the admiral a physical certificate proclaiming her an honorable "Daughter of Neptune" and a "Shellback."

With the admiral last, the five-hour ceremony was over. Beth stood, her muscles creaking, and announced the ceremony closed. She lifted the edge of her green skirt to try and wipe off the remaining grease.

One of the officers who had gone through the ceremony first came up to the admiral and quietly said something to her. The admiral nodded, then immediately left with a purpose, followed by her staff.

Fun was over, and it was back to the work at hand.

"Satan's Balls, girl," Mercy said, coming up to her. "Pretty gutsy with the admiral, there."

"What can she do? I was the queen."

"And now you're a deckhand, and she's the admiral. But good on you."

Beth stretched, leaning back. Her spine creaked.

"Not a bad day's work, though. You've never had so many boys and girls between your legs in your life."

"What?" Beth protested, snapping back forward.

"There," Mercy said, nodding between Beth's legs. "All those hot young bodies kneeling right there."

"Geeze, Mercy, is your mind always in the gutter?"

"Yeah, usually. You know that. But it's food for thought, you know? Didn't you even think about it? I mean, there are some hotties here, and you can use a little action. Do you some good."

"No, I didn't think like that. I'm not a cat in heat like you."

"Hey, I'm not like that anymore. I've got Rock."

"Yeah, just remember that, sista. You're taken," she said as she glanced up to where the some of the officers were chatting as some junior swabbies moved in to begin the clean up.

Commander Tuominen, as tall as he was, was easy to spot.

No, it wasn't like that. That was just a GT thing, nothing more.

She just had to keep telling herself that.

Chapter 4

"There he goes," Mercy said as they watched from the ready room as the scout took off. "Glad I'm not that poor sucker, all alone out there with just a mini-torp for protection. Fighter jocks rule, huh sista?"

Beth gave her a fist bump, but without conviction. Fighter jocks carried the same swagger as their 20th Century predecessors, but if there was a hierarchy, they occupied the next rung down from the scouts.

As a former corporate exploratory scout, Beth felt a degree of kinship with the scouts, not that she'd ever even met them. The task force had two of the secretive pilots, both former Wasp drivers, who strapped on their small Mosquito scouts, which were little more than engine and hull.

She was proud to be a fighter jock, and the thrill of combat made her feel alive. But there was also the thrill of going where no human had gone before, something she missed since joining the Navy.

Before the fight with the crystals broke out, the scouts had the most dangerous job in the Navy. Equipped with a barebones gate projector, they could make jumps into previously unexplored space . . . but with comparatively limited computational capabilities, mistakes—fatal mistakes— were relatively commonplace. Every year, one or two scouts were lost to the black.

Not that they were emplacing their own mini-gates for the task force, which would be too small for the capital ships. The task force had four GG-13 unmanned gate planters, which were linked, through the *Victory*, to the big fleet AIs back at First Fleet Headquarters on Refuge. But protocol was protocol, and with the task force making their approach to their target through a series of eight jumps, the far side of each one had to be checked before the *Victory* and her escorts would be given the green light to proceed.

Theoretically, the task force could make the voyage in a week at most, even considering the time it took for new gates to be emplaced. But with the scouts reconning each new section of space, the timeline was being stretched-out. And that called for a lot of dead time.

Which explained why the two fellow Wasp pilots were in the ready room.

"Just finish your class," Beth said. "I can't give mine until you're done with yours."

"This is fucking bullshit," Mercy said, slamming down her pad. "No one wants to listen to me prattle on about the Frandlinson Republic."

"Idle hands, idle minds and all," Beth said. "And I can't give my class on the rise of the Knights United until you set the stage. And it isn't like you're really doing any research. You're just downloading the class from the library."

Mercy sighed, then picked up her pad. "I still have to know what I'm presenting," she muttered.

With all the dead time, the junior pilots—petty officers and ensigns—were being given classes to teach the squadron's sailors. It was busy-work, both for the pilots and sailors, and everyone knew it. It was something that just had to be endured.

On the monitor, Beth could see the greenshirts already resetting the launch rail from the Mosquito launch. Somewhere, already kiloklicks away, a scout was about to make their way through the gate and into unexplored space, a pathfinder making sure the way was safe for the rest of them.

With a sigh, she looked back at her pad and returned to the Knights United order of battle.

Chapter 5

"Payback time," Mercy said as Fox shot through the mini-gate and started to move into their position in the Mendoza Sphere. "You got that right, sista," Beth said with conviction.

The Mendoza Sphere gave maximum coverage in three dimensions and was generally used when the enemy's location was uncertain. As of an hour ago, at least, the squadron knew there were at least 27 crystal ships at their objective.

How they'd located the FALs was why the Stingers were angry and calling for blood. Three hours before, an ore transport sent a distress call from an unoccupied section of space. The ship's crew hadn't been able to state the nature of their emergency before their distress call was cut off, so one of the two scouts, Lieutenant Commander Lettie "Ballerina" Smith, was dispatched to make contact and find out what had happened.

Immediately upon jumping into the system, Ballerina discovered the transport, or at least what had been a ship, scattered across the asteroid belt. Almost as quickly, she was set upon by the 27 crystal ships. She managed to get back her analytics as she tried to jump out of there, but the FALs took her out before she could escape.

Beth had seen the pilot around the ship, but she didn't really know her. Capgun, along with a few of the other pilots did, however, serving with Ballerina when she was a Wasp pilot. She didn't need to know her, though. The lieutenant commander was a Navy pilot, and losing her was the same as if she was in the squadron. Beth wanted to punish the crystals.

Normally, when a scout was lost, the mini-gate they used to jump was shut down for security reasons. This time, however, the admiral kept it open from their side. It was too small for a capital ship to pass through, but a Wasp was not that much larger than a scout. She ordered a rescue/punitive raid, scrambling the entire squadron. Beth hoped the scout pilot was alive, but she feared for her. The lieutenant commander had the same neck-cracker as the Wasp pilots, but her Mosquito didn't offer much protection.

Ten of the flights, forty Wasps, jumped through the minigate, leaving two flights on the near side for security. Forty Wasp pilots, all intent on wreaking havoc on the FALs.

With the forty fighter AIs in hive mode, all scanners working together and supplemented by the connection with the
Victory's battle AI, it didn't take long to locate the crystal ships in amongst the asteroid belt, as if they thought the metals would hide them.

"Fat chance, suckers," Beth muttered. They couldn't hide if they were inside a moon, much less than a bunch of rocks.

The commander ordered the squadron to shift to a Toriyama Cap, which projected power to the front as they sped forward to engage. Fox was below the orbital plane and to the far left, which meant they might not be as likely to engage, much to Mercy's annoyance, but this time, there were no M-57X's to give Beth or Wingnut priority.

There wasn't any sign of Ballerina, which wasn't good. But a detailed search was going to have to wait with the FALs ahead. They didn't charge out to meet the Stingers, but the threat could not be ignored.

So, this is going to be a close in-fight.

Which was fine with Beth. The Battle of Toowoomba had been close-in as well, and while the Stingers had lost some good pilots, the planet and station had been saved.

The FALs were not rushing out to meet them. On one level, there was no tremendous difference if one fighter was still while another approached. Closing speed was the same for both. However, giving up speed meant giving up maneuverability, and for torpedoes, that meant giving up on initial velocity.

Not that the FALs were sitting still. They were moving around in tight loops within the asteroid belt, giving them some speed, but forcing the Stingers to approach through open space to reach them.

"Shift course," Gollum said as a new course appeared on Beth's display. It looked like they were going to try and get behind the asteroid belt, to cut off any escape.

"Hell fuck!" Mercy snarled into her mic. "We're getting cut out of the action?"

"Calm down," Gollum told her. "No one is cutting us off."

"Really, sir? Then why are we getting sent off to bumfuck nowhere?"

"Mercy, let it go," Beth passed on the S2S.

"Easy for you to say," her friend muttered before cutting out of the net.

Beth didn't like the shift, either, but for a different reason. It would be difficult getting into any kind of blocking position in time to do any good. She didn't like to second-guess the commander, but she thought he'd made a mistake. Better to gain immediate numerical superiority and with interlocking, mutually supporting fields of fire. Every Wasp should have another covering their six.

As always, the waiting was the hardest. Beth watched her display as the deadly ballet began to coalesce. A few of the crystal ships, as if unable to hold back, fired, but to no effect. The Stingers kept up their relentless advance, holding their fire as the two forces closed.

And then, the floodgates opened. A couple of hundred kiloklicks out, Charlie and Echo opened up with a barrage of torps and energy cannons. Immediately, the FALs responded in kind, and the battle was on.

Beth watched as they raced to get into position, keeping in check her desire to fire. The first torpedo reached the FALs, hitting one of the crystal ships that had ventured too far forward.

"Get some!" Beth shouted.

Another torpedo detonated, but against one of the asteroids. A FAL pilot, displaying nerves (or whatever they had) of steel had let the torpedo track it, scooting behind the asteroid at the last second.

Beth frowned. Something so simple should not have happened. An M-57 was too sophisticated for that to work. Something else had to have affected it.

Before she could follow that train of thought, Redeye and the *Georgie* exploded. One moment, she was barreling in, P-13 blazing, and the next, she was a mist of space junk.

"Holy shit, did you see that?" Mercy asked.

Beth stared at her display in shock. There hadn't been a warning. No torpedoes, no energy weapon fire. One moment, Redeye was there, the next moment, she wasn't.

Her AI lit up with a mine warning. It hadn't identified any, but calculated a 72% probability that it was a mine that had taken out Redeye.

But the FALs haven't used mines before, she protested to herself before she considered it.

Humans used mines. The Stingers had used them on their first battle with the FALs, in fact. They were small, relatively difficult to detect, and effective. Their disadvantage was that they had to be in place in the path of the oncoming enemy.

Beth slapped herself in the front of her helmet. *Of course, they knew we would be coming to them.*

Stupid assumption that they didn't use mines. The concept was not a particularly difficult one, evidently to crystalline life as well as human.

In the face of the threat, Commander Tuominen immediately changed the plan. Fox, Kilo, and Bravo were to pour energy fire into space in the path of the squadron. They were minesweepers now.

"If our P-13's will even set them off," Mercy said over the S2S.

Beth loved Mercy dearly, but her wingman's negative attitude was beginning to wear on her. The commander had to do something, and his AI most likely gave this action the highest probability of success.

Within moments, Beth received an assigned sector to blanket. Her targeting program wanted something to fire at, but she overrode the AI and started sweeping the area, an eye on her readouts. Sustained firing like this was both a drain on her power as well as a huge heat producer. In the vacuum of space, getting rid of heat was one of the biggest problems the Wasps had.

Another Wasp was taken out, Lieutenant "Nose" Grimore and the *Blue Ghost*. That was two Wasps lost, and they hadn't even closed with the enemy yet. Beth gritted her teeth and continued to pour gigajoules of energy into her assigned sector.

She couldn't think about Nose now, who'd only five days ago found out he was a new father. She had to push that aside. But she felt detached, almost guilty. The *Tala* hadn't even been touched so far, and her shields were still at 100%. Yet most of her fellow fighters were taking fire. More than just taking fire— Redeye and Nose . . .

Snap out of it. Time for that later. Focus, Floribeth!

Several explosions registered on her display . . . but no more Wasps were hit. Evidently, the counter-mine fire was having an effect. Not for Beth, though. No mines detonated in her sector as she poured energy into it, her temps rising to redline levels.

Beth kept up the fire, but shifted into the asteroid belt proper as the lead elements closed the distance.

"Auto-avoid," the commander passed ten seconds before the Charlie Flight reached the outer edges of the asteroid belt.

Unlike as depicted in the holovids, an asteroid belt was not a jumble of closely packed rocks, all bouncing around like ancient bumper cars. There was open space between most of the larger asteroids with smaller particles and microdust filling in. Each of the Wasps had repeller fields that pushed away the smaller particles, allowing the fighter to "slip through," even at high speeds. However, the repellers were less effective as the particles became larger, and at high speeds, pilots were simply not able to react fast enough to avoid the larger rocks. The autoavoid left control of the Wasp to her pilot, but shifted 22% of the fighter's scanners to identify any potential threat and override the navigation to avoid it. Entering a close-in dogfight with the extremely maneuverable FALs with 22% of the scanners otherwise occupied was not the preferred way to fight, but it beat hitting a 5-ton chunk of ice and rock at speed.

As Charlie, then Echo blasted into the belt, the FALs started a crazy, disjointed pattern of movement. None of it made any sense to Beth nor the Navy AIs. Charlie Flight scored two quick kills as the FALs jitterbugged around, one with a railgun. Including Beth's kill, that was only the second time a crystal ship had been splashed with one.

"What the hell are they doing? Are they crazy?" Capgun asked over the flight net.

Beth didn't understand the FALs. No one, not even the xenopsychologists, really did. But they were rational, thinking beings. The mines were new, and they had splashed Nose and Redeye. Their positioning within the asteroid belt, almost assuredly coupled with something else yet unknown, had defeated a torpedo. The FALs knew how to adjust, to change tactics. So as sure as Aria has three moons, Beth knew that whatever they were doing had a purpose. She just didn't know what that purpose was.

Sometimes, the fog of war couldn't be dispersed. Warriors simply had to push forward and hope skill and luck would prevail. This was one of those times. Pilots flew their Wasps into the asteroid belt to take the fight to the FALs.

The tide was turning. The FALs had shown a new face, and that had cost the Stingers, but the remaining Navy pilots were adjusting. They might not be the disciplined unit, working in unison as they'd been trained to do, but even in a melee, the humans were beginning to take control.

Beth didn't like that they'd abandoned their coordinated fighting. For a pilot who's gotten her start out alone in the black for weeks on end, she'd gotten used to having wingmen with her, covering her six. Now, with only Mercy as a wingman, she felt exposed.

The *Tala's* alarm sounded. One of the remaining FALs snapped out of its weird widdershins dance and fired a brace of two torpedoes at them. The two pilots immediately targeted the incoming with their cannons as Beth fed in the close-in defense data to her railgun. It never got that far. Both torpedoes were taken out beyond ass-puckering range.

The FAL flickered them, for lack of a better term, with its energy cannon. Not enough to do any damage, but enough for the two Wasps' alarms to go off. Beth could swear it was waiting, begging them to engage.

If that's what you want, you've got it, she thought, targeting it with her M-57.

"I've got the fucker," Mercy said, firing her second torp, beating Beth to the punch.

Beth backed off from firing hers. If Mercy splashed the FAL, all the better, but despite the overall course the battle had taken, she knew the AIs needed more data to make sense of what was happening to the torpedoes within the belt. She'd hold off in hopes the AIs could crack what was going on.

But she could still pour fire into the crystal ship. Her P-13 was showing signs of the heavy load by now. Heat dissipation was suffering, and her efficiency levels had dropped by eight points. That would continue to get worse as she pushed the cannon to its limits.

Sorry about that, Josh. You're just going to have to switch out the Esptein coil when I get back.

The Navy didn't give her the hadron cannon to baby it. It was meant to be used. That's why they had spares back on the *Victory.*

The FAL jinked impossibly to the right, Mercy's torp still locked on. But Beth had seen this before. It was leading the M57 to another hunk of rock. Mercy has seen it, too, and with a shout of inarticulate rage, she adjusted course to close directly with the FAL just before the torpedo detonated harmlessly. Another FAL broke off its weird widdershins rotation and started to slide forward. Its beamer reached out, taking Mercy under fire.

"Mercy!" Beth shouted as she shifted fire to the second FAL.

"Keep that bastard piece-of-shit off me while I splash this mother-fucker," Mercy said as she ignored the second FAL and poured her fire into the first.

"Red Devil, watch your shields," Gollum passed on the flight net.

Beth shifted her gaze to the order of battle. The lieutenant commander and Capgun had lost their target but were not too far off. It looked like they were turning to come back to join them.

"I'm OK. Still holding strong," Mercy said.

"Mercy, you've still got another 57," Beth said. "Use it."

"Not yet while it can still dodge. I'm going to ram it down its fucking throat. Just keep that other one off of me."

Hell, Mercy, just let it go, Beth silently pleaded as she pulled up the *Louhi's* vitals. Under the combined fire of two crystal ships, her shields were dropping like rocks.

Everything was happening too quickly. Space battles were slow moving, fought at long distances. By pulling the Stingers into the asteroid belt, however, the FALs had changed the formula, forcing the Navy fighters out of their comfort zone.

And now a FAL had goaded Mercy into a mad charge, like a jousting knight of old. Beth didn't know what to do other than try to break the second FALs fire onto her wingman. She snapped off one of her 57's, hoping that, combined with her beamer fire, it would make the FAL shift off of Mercy and onto her.

"Hamlin, break off!" the flight leader ordered Mercy. "Now!"

"I'm almost there," Mercy passed. "Just a few more seconds."

"Look at your shields! You don't have a few more seconds."

The lieutenant was right. Something had failed inside of the *Louhi*, and her shield strength was plummeting far too quickly.

"Roger that. I see it. Oh, fuck," she said as she fired her last torpedo.

Instead of breaking off, though, she continued forward, pouring beamer fire into the FAL, which finally seemed to blink.

It shifted its fire to Mercy's torpedo while jinking again.

"That's right sucker!" Mercy crowed as the torpedo detonated . . . and an instant before her shields failed and her fighter went dead.

Chapter 6

"No, Mercy!" Beth screamed into her mic as the *Louhi*'s icon on her display went black.

Rage overtook her, and she lashed out, sending another torpedo after the second FAL, and redlining her cannon. Almost immediately, her target shifted fire to Beth as she charged forward. The FAL kept up the fire as it adjusted its own course for a denser pack of asteroid rubble.

Whatever was affecting the Navy torpedoes sent hers offtarget. No matter. She still had her cannon, even at a degraded efficiency. She still had her rail gun. She'd splashed a FAL with it before. She could do it again.

If she was going to use her railgun, Beth needed to splash it before the FAL could reach the potential cover of the rubble. She kept her agony at bay, focusing every gram of her being on killing the crystal fucker who'd killed her best friend.

So focused was she on her target that she didn't understand when it exploded. One minute, she was watching the range close as she ran firing solutions, and the next it was gone.

She stared dumbly at her display for a moment until Gollum broke in with, "Check on Mercy."

He and Capgun were still inbound, they were close enough that the flight leader had splashed her target. She felt cheated a moment, angry that he'd taken away her chance for revenge.

For Mercy . . .

Wait. What did he say?

"Mercy's dead. I saw it."

"No, the *Louhi's* dead. Mercy's still alive."

A surge of hope swept through her. The *Louhi* was dead on her screen, but Beth didn't have all of the readings. As flight leader, Gollum would. She slaved into his display, and there, Mercy's bios showed that she was still alive. Barely.

Her lifeline was the yellow of being on life support. Yellow wasn't good, but it meant she was wasn't dead yet.

She maxed out the compensators bringing the *Tala* around.

Capgun and Gollum were closing in on the first FAL, the one Mercy had targeted. Her torpedo hadn't splashed it, something Beth only noted in passing as she kept her eyes glued on the blip on her display that was Mercy. She tried switching to a visual, but all she could see was a tiny speck of light as she started to match trajectory.

Where before, she thought the battle was being rushed, now things slowed to a crawl. The FALs were breaking contact, and the battle had shifted to a pursuit. The net was alive with excitement, pilots referring to the fight now as a turkey shoot.

Quite a few of her fellow pilots were getting their first kills.

One fleeing FAL passed within 300 kiloklicks of her as she closed with her friend, but that barely registered with her. Two pilots from Lima gleefully chased it down while Gollum and Capgun provided security.

She could have G-Shot and zipped past Mercy in minutes, but that wouldn't do much good. She had to get close enough to activate the grappling beam. It took too long, but finally, she could see the *Louhi* on her visuals. The ship looked undamaged. Only the readings revealed that she was DIS—Dead in Space. Outside of the asteroid belt, she'd continue on forever. Inside, there was the risk of a collision. Already, the dust and microparticles would be abrading away the skin of the fighter. Beth had to get her out of there before she collided with something more substantial.

Beth took off her neck-cracker and peered through her canopy as she slid into position on Mercy and the *Louhi*. Most pilots might go through their entire career without seeing another fighter close-up while out in the black. The distances were just too great. This was Beth's second time, however. The first time had been when she'd rescued Bull after the Battle of SG-9222.

She couldn't see inside the *Louhi's* canopy. "Can you hear me, sista?" Beth asked, not expecting an answer. She didn't get one.

"I'm here with Mercy. I'm about to get into position to grapple," she passed on the flight net.

"Roger that. Keep me informed," Gollum responded.

A Wasp could activate the grappling beam from any aspect, but it worked best when the two fighters were belly-to-belly.
Unlike the powerful tractors on the capital ships, the Wasp had their poor cousins, which could be broken with power surges or severe course corrections. A belly-to-belly aspect maximized the connection. Beth started rotating around, sliding into position.

"I've got you sista. Ready to take you back," she passed on the slight chance that Mercy could somehow hear her.

Just as she was about to activate the beam, the *Tala* changed course, knocking the two out of alignment.

What the . . .?

When she took off her neck-cracker, she'd left it connected, so her canopy HUD wasn't on. She pulled the hardwire, and the display lit up. A blue-flashing light told the story. Nothing was wrong. It was just that the auto-avoid had kicked on.

"Oh, shit!" she said as that sunk in.

With the auto-avoid making the adjustment, there were no collision alarms. She had to ask for the Proximity Display, and there, in the yellow cone of caution, was a 12-ton chunk of rock. She was in the clear . . . but Mercy in the *Louhi* was not, and collision would be in 13 seconds.

"Fire Ant, you're—" Gollum started before Beth tuned him out.

She had to figure out something, but there was no time. It took a good 30 seconds to implement the grapple, and that was if she was still in the correct position. She started to power-up her rail gun, hoping to blast the rock into pieces, but she didn't have the location and it would take a couple of steps to mesh the Proximity Display with her Fire Mission AI.

Her subconscious knew what she had to do before her conscious mind could work its way through its decision tree. She turned off the auto-avoid and took over manual control of the *Tala.* She'd drifted a good hundred meters from her former position, a miniscule distance in space, too far for the few seconds left to her.

She crossed herself, muttering an "Ave Maria" as she steered the *Tala* into the *Louhi,* praying that the Wasps could take the impact.

"Beth! No!" Capgun shouted over the net.

Mercy's fighter seemed to rush at her. She instinctively flinched, and Beth braced for the collision as the two collided. The *Tala* didn't break apart, and the compensators dampened most of the shock, if not the loud clang that filled the cockpit. She pulled back, taking advantage of the rebound as the time to impact reached zero . . . and she was clear. It had to be her imagination, but she would swear to her dying days that she caught a glimpse of the rock as she shot by.

But what about the *Louhi?* She spun the *Tala* around and craned her neck, trying to spot her friend, but seeing nothing. Panic started taking over.

She switched her display over, and to her relief, there was the *Louhi,* two klicks away and drifting farther.

"Nice thinking, Fire Ant," Gollum said. "Now go get her."

"Shit, girl, that took brass cajones," Capgun passed on the S2S.

Beth giggled in relief. Giggled like a five-year-old girl. "Sorry, Capgun. No cajones here," she said, leaning her head back and closing her eyes as her heart started to beat normally again.

"Bigger than I've got. Much bigger. Now, go get her." He waited a moment, then said, "Big cajones or not, we're tied again. Four each."

It took her a moment to register what he was saying. He must have splashed the surviving FAL of the two, the one Mercy has targeted.

She laughed, glad that enemy fighter, which had somehow slipped her mind, wasn't around. Her brain was too numb to think of a snappy comeback, so she simply said, "Eat me," the all-purpose response.

But she couldn't dawdle. They'd escaped one collision, but there were more rocks out there, bigger rocks. She left the autoavoid off, but brought the Promixity Display to primacy, expanding the warning to one minute. That was pushing the capabilities of her little scanner for smaller, 10 kg-sized rocks, but she wanted as much advanced warning as possible.

Beth quickly closed the distance. Her cockpit facing the *Louhi's* belly. It was scratched, but Beth couldn't see any significant damage. Beth whispered thanks to the good folks at Kyocera Aerospace for making the Wasps so sturdy.

She rotated the Tala again for a belly-to-belly presentation, checked the alignment, then turned on the grapple. She could hear, almost feel the hum as the small cymaclon spun up, sending out its field to excite the molecules in the *Louhi's* receptor plate. Twenty-seven seconds later, the LED flashed green, and the connection strength appeared on her display. Her job now was to make sure the bar never went below 75 T, risking a break in the grapple.

"I've got a lock," she passed to Gollum.

"Go ahead and take her back. I've already cleared it with the commander."

Beth took a moment to study the order of battle. The Stingers had taken some damage. Serious damage. Six Wasps were lost. Two were being towed back to the gate, hopefully with the other pilot, like Mercy, still alive. But the rest were swarming the remaining few crystal ships.

The FALs had tried something new. It seemed that like humans, they were attempting to figure out better ways to fight. The Stingers had been able to meet the new threat and win out, but at a very steep price. Maybe too high. After she got back, when things calmed down, the loss would hit her. But for now, she had to keep all of that at bay. She still had a job to do.

With a sigh, she started slowly changing course, mindful of the T-numbers as she pulled the *Louhi* with her. It was time to get Mercy back to the *Victory*.

Chapter 7

"It was a close call, but she'll pull through," the ship's surgeon told the three of them. "Not before some regenerative therapy, though."

Beth winced. For all the advances of modern medicine, regenerating damaged nerves had to be done the old way, and the old way was decidedly painful.

"The new helmets shielded most of her brain, but below the neck, there was extensive nerve damage."

"At least the neck-crackers were good for something," Capgun muttered.

Half his size, Beth hated them, too, but for once, Jean Luc and his R&D-types had come up with something effective. If this fight had happened before the neck-crackers were issued, Mercy would be dead. Right then and there, Beth swore that she wasn't going to complain about them ever again.

"How long will she be in here?" Gollum asked the doc.

"Here? Another day or so, I'd be guessing."

"What? Only another day. But I thought you said she'd be going through therapy. Not in a day," the lieutenant commander said, his eyebrows scrunched together in confusion.

She's getting sent back, Beth realized. *They can't do that here.*

The surgeon looked equally confused at the Fox Flight leader.

Beth put her hand on his arm and tugged him close, then said, "They're medivacing her off the ship."

"Well, of course, we are," the surgeon said, overhearing her. "We're already prepping her, but they can do much better at Refuge. Less time and with better monitoring."

"Can we see her?" Capgun asked.

The ship's surgeon looked them up and down, lips forming to say no when Beth interrupted, "She's my wingman and best friend, sir. And she's engaged to my brother. She'll want to see me before she goes."

The surgeon glanced over to the lieutenant who nodded in confirmation. He frowned, then grudgingly said, "You're not sterile. Put on an isolation suit, and I'll let you go in. With the V-prep, she's extremely vulnerable to infections right now.

"Les, can you get them the suits?" he asked one of the nurses.

Three minutes later, with the white isolation suits over their flightsuits, the three were let in the airlock. Mercy looked tiny, lying in the hospital bed, tubes running from under a single sheet and to a large, impressive-looking piece of medical something-or-other. Beside the machine, another white-suited man sat.

Mercy's eyes were closed, but she opened them as the three approached.

"Satan's balls," she croaked out. "You look like three ghosts. But since one of you is about waist-high to a wallaby, I'm guessing that's you, Beth, with Capgun and the lieutenant? Am I right?"

Beth stepped up and reached out an enclosed hand to put on her friend's arm.

As she leaned in, Mercy could see through the face shield, and a small smile creased her face.

"How are you feeling, sista?"

"Like shit. That fucking FAL fried my ass."

"Well, you held on it for long enough. I kept yelling at you to break. I had your six."

"I had lock. I figured all I had to do was outlast its shields, and I'd splash the fucker without taking damage myself."

"You figured wrong," Gollum said, but without anger. "We thought we'd lost you."

"I'm too tough for that," Mercy said. "Well, not that tough, I guess," she added, gesturing at the medical equipment.

"Did I get him, at least? My mind is kinda fuzzy right now. I know I fired my 57 there at the end, but after that . . ." she trailed off.

Beth looked over at Gollum. They had debated on the way over what to say. It was possible that Mercy had damaged the
FAL, but she hadn't splashed it. Capgun had. It wasn't likely that she'd be getting credit once the analysts went through everything.

He shook his head.

"I don't think so, Mercy. But we're waiting for the analysts.
They'll be able to tell."

Mercy closed her eyes and was quiet for a moment, and Beth wondered if she had fallen asleep.

"Did you get another kill?" Mercy asked softly.

"Fire Ant brought you back after you were taken out,"
Capgun said. "Took herself out of the fight."

"You were primed, Beth. First ace and all."

"For what? Without my wingman?" Beth asked, thankful for the isolation suit that hid the blush she could feel taking over her face.

Mercy reached over and took her hand, giving it a weak squeeze.

"The Doc says you're getting medivaced back to civilization," Beth said, anxious to change the subject. "You'll be living large at the Naval Hospital, all the comforts of home."

"Yeah, going through nerve regen," Mercy said with a small shudder. She knew what she was facing. "Not my idea of living large.

"This stuff's bad enough," she said, nodding at the machine to which she was hooked.

"Does it hurt?" Beth asked.

"No, not really. I can't feel much below my neck at all. I guess that's one good thing about getting my nerves fried. But that stuff they're pumping me up with, the V-prep, it's like I'm itching from the inside out."

Capgun stepped closer and pointed at the two tubes running from the machine to under the sheet at waist level. "Where the heck do they connect that to? I mean, not your . . ."

Mercy shrugged and said, "Like I told you, I can't feel anything."

"To her femoral artery. Left one in, the right one out," the med tech said from beside the machine, the first time he'd opened his mouth since they'd arrived.

"Doesn't make much difference to me where . . ." Mercy said before trailing off and closing her eyes.

"I think that's enough," the tech said. "She's gone through a lot."

Beth wasn't ready to leave, and she looked to Gollum, but he nodded and tilted his head toward the hatch.

"You get better, now, Mercy," she said, giving her friend's shoulder a squeeze. "I need my wingman."

Mercy opened her eyes and grabbed Beth's hand before she could pull away. "Don't wait for me. You get that fifth kill first, Beth. Don't let any of the guys beat you to ace. Estrogen all the way, sista."

"You got it sista," she said as Mercy closed her eyes again, her hand dropping free.

Chapter 8

"Well, that's that," Wingnut said, hurrying to catch up to her as they filed out of the briefing room.

"Yeah, we're going back."

"Think any of the Scorpions are going to beat us now?"

Beth hadn't even considered that when they were told the mission was being cut short, and if judging by the groans when Captain Restov made the announcement, he wasn't the only one who was upset. Their mission had been to take it to the FALs, and while they'd had limited success, there had been nothing major, nothing to cheer about. And the limited success had come at a heavy cost, at least among the pilots.

But with six Wasps and a Mosquito pilot lost, with five more Wasps deadlined beyond the *Victory's* ability to repair, and with the *Mary O'Reilly*, one of the task force's destroyers having drive problems, the First Fleet Commander had pulled the plug.

Probably not First Fleet. This had to come from Navy HQ.

With Wingnut looking at her expectantly, she slowed down. Wingnut, Capgun, and she had four kills each. Another four pilots had three. But by cutting this mission short, all of them would probably be stuck where they were for a while.

The captain had also told them that Task Force Iron Sword, with VX-22 aboard, was going to take their place, pushing out the security ring into the inner spiral.

"Anyone there have any numbers?" she asked him.

"Reina Duarte and Laz Dickenson. Three each."

Beth knew about Lieutenant Commander Reina "Queen" Duarte, the Scorpions' XO. She had the rep as a good, aggressive pilot. She didn't know much about this Dickenson guy, though.

Beth hadn't really bought into the hype over who was going to make ace first . . . she thought. Now that they were going back and the Scorpions were going out, she felt . . . she didn't know what she felt. Disappointment? Jealousy?

Whatever she felt, she didn't like it. This wasn't a game. Too many people had died fighting the FALs. Mercy had been so driven to just get one kill that she'd pushed the envelope and was sitting in a hospital ward right now going through therapy.

And she was lucky. She could have easily been killed.

"If they do, they do. All for the cause, right? That's bigger than any single pilot," she said, looking him right in the eyes.

"Yeah, of course," Wingnut hurriedly agreed. "Just curious, that's all. As long as the mission is accomplished."

"Right. Well, I'm going to see how Josh is progressing with the *Tala*. You never know. We might get a mission on the way back. If not, I'll see you back at fleet," she said, turning to head to the hangar spaces.

The mission was paramount. She knew that. She embraced that. Not personal achievement. It didn't matter who made ace first.

Still . . .

Chapter 9

"Hey, Mercy. How're things?" Beth asked as her friend's haggard image appeared on the screen.

"Been better, sista, been better. This . . . this shit sucks big time," she said, sweeping a hand to indicate her body. "Remind me to never get my nerves fried again."

"Only two more weeks, right? Then another month of convalescent leave."

"*Only* two more weeks? When you're getting tortured, two weeks is a hell of a long time."

"Yeah, I know. Sorry about that."

"Not your fault. It's the fucking penny-pincher's fault," she said with a scowl. "They could have saved me all of this."

Beth kept her face expressionless. This was Mercy's latest bitch. If the neck-crackers saved her brain, she reasoned, then why didn't they use the same tech to protect her entire body?

Why limit it to just her head?

That made sense on the surface, at least. But there was more to it. The counteracting fields were extremely limited in reach, breaking down if they were stretched beyond about 35 centimeters, and the brains of the system were extremely expensive. Between the pilot's helmet and the ship's AI cocoon, they cost more than a complete Wasp. And while the neckcracker undoubtedly saved Mercy's life, they were not completely effective . . . just look at the six pilots lost in the last mission.

Beth knew that the science-types were working to improve the efficacy and reach of the fields, but that would take some time, and then more time to field the units. It wasn't going to be done tomorrow.

Still, she knew what Mercy had been going through as her nerves were stimulated into regenerating themselves.

No, actually, I don't. Recovery from G-Shot is nothing like what she's going through.

"But, I'm glad you called. I've got something to tell you."

"You asked me to," Beth said. "So, here I am, at zero-darkthirty."

With the *Victory* back in system, it was synched to First Fleet Headquarters time, so it was the same early morning hour for Mercy. Maybe she was just getting done with another treatment.

"We've got something to tell you, I mean."

"We?" Beth wondered. *Who's this "we?"*

Mercy leaned forward and touched her display. A moment later, Rocky's image appeared at the bottom of her screen. Which answered that question, and the time. She did a quick calculation. It was almost 11 at night back home in San Miguel. What it didn't answer was why Rocky needed to be in on the call.

"Hey, Rocky," Beth said, frowning slightly.

"Hey, Beth," he said.

"So, what is it you two have to tell me?"

Beth knew that Rocky had tried to make it to Refuge to visit Mercy during her treatments, but with the cost of interstellar travel, that had been put on hold. They'd decided to hold off, and Mercy would take her leave back on New Cebu.

Has that changed?

Mercy looked a little embarrassed, which was weird. The woman had no shame and few social graces, never caring what others thought about her. She was never unsure of herself or embarrassed. That was one of the things that Beth loved about her.

"Like you said, I'm supposed to be done with this freaking nerve regen in two weeks."

Beth suppressed a smile. If Rocky weren't on the call, Mercy would have said "fucking nerve regen." Evidently, Mercy cared what *one* person thought of her language usage.

"And I'm going to spend my leave with your family. So, we're thinking, what with the situation and all, uh, that . . . I mean . . ."

"Beth, we're getting married," Rocky said.

Beth's mouth dropped open in shock.

"You're *what*?"

"We're getting married. On the 17th," he said.

Beth looked at Mercy, who's face broke out into a radiant smile.

"Yeah, sista. Rocky and me are getting hitched. Me! Can you imagine it?"

Beth didn't know what to say. She knew they were getting closer, and the possibility of having Mercy as a sister-in-law had crossed her mind. But now? While they'd been communicating via the commercial comms since the day they'd met, they'd *physically* been together for only six or seven days so far. How could that be enough time?

"I . . . congratulations?" she said, unable to keep her rising tone from making it a question rather than a statement.

"Oh, yes, she's taking it well," Rocky said, a knowing smile turning up the corners of his mouth.

"No, I mean it. Congratulations," Beth said more assuredly. "I'm happy for you."

"I hear a 'but' in there," Rocky said.

"No. Well, maybe. I mean, are you two ready for this? You haven't known each other that long."

"No, we haven't. But if it's right, it's right. And given the circumstances, it may be a long, long time before there's another opportunity," Mercy said. "And I love him. I can't wait for who knows how long. Or even if . . ."

Or if you'll survive the war, Beth mentally finished off Mercy's sentence.

And she was right. The chances were that neither of the two pilots would survive if the war dragged on, which it looked like it would. If Mercy could grab a little happiness before that, then why not? Who was she to object?

"You're right. You two deserve some happiness, and if this is your only shot, then grab it."

"Thanks, sista. I'm happy to hear you say that. And since, you're, you know, the situation, we're thinking maybe you can come. Be my maid of honor. If you like that kind of thing."

Beth glanced down at the spy eye. The light remained green. Mercy hadn't come right out and said that the *Victory* was back in port, but Big Brother was always listening in, and you never knew what might set him off.

"I . . . I'd be honored," Beth said, realizing it was true. She'd have never guessed that irreverent Mercy would ever get married, much less with a traditional ceremony, but if she were, Beth would love to be part of it. "But I'm not sure I can get leave."

The task force might be back in port refitting and getting upgrades, but the entire Navy was still on a war footing, and normal leave was suspended for the duration. Even in the yards, they were on a 24-hour alert status, ready to deploy again to meet any threat.

"We know you can't spend time, but if you can even swing a couple of hours, we would love to have you here."

Beth thought about it a moment. Refuge was at a gate nexus. She could take a commercial liner to make the direct jump to New Cebu. Over and back, she could probably make it in 20 hours. That would give her about two hours for the wedding.

The question was whether she could get a day's leave approved.

As if reading her mind, Mercy said, "You've got friends in high places. I'm sure they can swing it."

Beth wasn't so sure about that. She knew the commander had her back, but the commodore? Having four kills didn't mean squat with her. It was worth a try, though.

"I'd love to be there, of course. Can't let my little brother and best friend get hitched without me. I'll try to get leave. I can't promise anything, but I can try."

"Thanks, sista. That's all we can ask."

Beth started feeling a flush of excitement. Weddings were big things on New Cebu, not just for the couple getting married, but for the entire community. And this one was for family.

"Have you told *ina* yet?" she asked Rocky.

"No, we wanted to tell you, first."

"Well, you'd better get on it, boy. The 17th? She's got only three weeks to pull this off? Time's a wasting!"

A wedding normally was a year in planning. Three weeks was nothing. But if anyone could put it together, their mother could.

The big question for her was if she could get the leave.

Chapter 10

"Shit!" she shouted in the empty passage as she angrily strode back to the squadron spaces. "The bitch!"

Bryson Hemp, the admin clerk had given her the heads up.

The admiral herself had denied her leave.

One friggin day, and she couldn't give me that.

The command master chief looked up as she marched past, then quickly looked back at her pad, not wanting to catch Beth's eyes. She didn't care. This was for the commander.

She rapped on the open hatch, then announced, "Petty Officer Second Class Dalisay, to see the squadron commander as ordered."

"Enter," Commander Tuominen said from behind his desk. Beth marched up and centered herself in front of him.

"It's about your leave request, Dalisay," he started before taking in the fire flaring from her eyes. "I see the word has already reached you. But to make it official, Admiral Nzama has disapproved your leave request."

"Can we send it up to Fleet, sir?" she asked, trying to hold herself together.

"No, we can't. It's the admiral's call."

"This is bullshit . . . sir."

The commander's eyebrows lifted ever-so-slightly at her uncharacteristic outburst.

And it was uncharacteristic. But while she knew her chances of getting the leave approved were small, she'd started to get excited about it once the *Victory* had returned to Refuge.

Actually, she was a little torn. Mercy was her best friend, and Rocky was her little brother. Some irrational part of her, deep inside her psyche, worried that with them together, she

Jonathan P. Brazee

might be losing out as they focus on each other. But for the most part, she was excited. Helping with the planning, even longdistance, had enthused her. She wanted to go. She *had* to go.

"In case you've forgotten, Petty Officer, we're at war."

"I know, sir. But the *Victory's* got her launch rails disassembled. Even if we got the call, it'd take the full 24 hours to get that operational, maybe more. What harm can it do? I just don't get it. After all I've—"

"After you've what, Petty Officer?" he snapped, steel in his voice. "After you've sacrificed? Like Lieutenant Hadley? Like Lister? Don't you tell me what you've done here in the squadron."

Beth blanched. He was right, of course. She'd been lucky. Swordfish, Hurl, the others. They'd given up their lives. And here she was pouting like a little girl. She was being selfish. Mercy and Rocky didn't need her there. Being at the wedding was for *her*, and now she was upset because the admiral was taking that away from her. The *war* was taking that away from her.

She stood quietly for a long moment, then feeling mortified, said, "Aye-aye, sir. I understand. May I be dismissed?"

"Yes, you may."

She came to attention, performed an about-face, and started to march out when the commander said, "Wait a moment, Petty
Officer."

"Sir?" she asked, turning back around.

"AT3 Frye said something about the *Tala's* synch comb. I want you to make sure your fighter is ready to go.

"Sir?" she asked again.

This was the first she'd heard about anything wrong with the *Tala*. And if there was something wrong, why did the commander know about it before she did?

"Your fighter's synch comb," he said as if she should be aware of what was going on. "If it's giving you problems, I want that fixed now while we're here in the yards."

The synch comb was a small, but vital part of the *Tala*. It acted as a traffic controller, enabling all parts of the fighter to mesh seamlessly with each other. If it were out of whack, then the *Tala* would not function at peak performance. If the comb were too far gone, the fighter would cease functioning at all.

At 0.05% variance, regulations were that the fighter would be deadlined, and then the comb had to be reset and synched again. The Wasp would then take some routine jumps before it was greenlighted as combat operational.

The problem was that this was the first Beth had heard about it. She wanted to ask for more information, but she also didn't want to admit that she wasn't aware of the situation, however, and look like she out of the loop.

"Yes, sir," she said, keeping it simple. "I'm on it."

"As you should be. I don't want to have another Wasp on the deadlined report. So, get it up. And unless we go into Alpha, you still have to check-flight it. I'd recommend Washburne IV and the Huang Training Area, but that's up to you."

Beth stared hard at the commander for a moment, but he was looking back down at his pad, obviously dismissing her. The commander normally didn't get down into the weeds, and that was a lot of detail for him to be giving her. The HTA was not the normal training area for First Fleet. Not that it mattered much from a practical standpoint. Empty space was empty space, after all. It was just a weird suggestion, and suggestions from a CO usually carried the weight of orders.

"Aye-aye, sir," she said, spinning back around and marching out of his office.

She ignored the Command Master Chief and stormed down the passage. She was going to bite off half of a certain AT3's ass.

Chapter 11

"Josh! What the hell's going on? Why am I finding out from the CO that the *Tala's* synch comb is wonky," she asked as she strode up on her plane captain, his head buried in the Wasp's access hatch.

"I don't know that it is," he said, dropping his head lower and out of the fuselage so he could see her. "That's why I'm checking."

With that, he straightened up, and his head disappeared back inside.

What the . . .

"Josh, I need to know if the *Tala* is down!" she said, a little taken aback by his attitude.

She bent over and sidled over to join him, looking up to where he had his multiscan linked to readouts.

"Is the comb synch OK or not?" she asked.

"I'm getting a variable reading, from point-zero-two to point-zero-four," he said.

"Which is within acceptable parameters," she said, relieved. She was still angry that the CO had to be the one to tell her, but at least the *Tala* was combat operational.

"Maybe," he said, "But I don't like how it's bouncing about.
I think I'm going to run a trickle test tomorrow."

"What? A trickle test? Why?"

New fighters underwent a trickle test, which slowed down the analytics process to glacial speeds, which then allowed for greater accuracy in base readings and synchronization. Wasps already in use almost never underwent the tests, unless the FC engine had been replaced.

"I'd just feel better doing it, to be sure she's all right," he said.

"But you said the *Tala* was within tolerances," she said, thinking back to the CO telling her he didn't want her Wasp on the deadlined list.

"As plane captain, I'm calling it," he said with conviction.

Which was his right. Either the plane captain or the pilot could down-check a fighter, and the other could not countermand that. But that didn't mean Beth had to like it. All thoughts of missing Mercy's wedding had fled as she confronted her plane captain.

"That's going to deadline her for at least two days," she protested.

"Take a look up here," he said, pointing farther inside the fuselage.

She stood up, her head just inside the access panel, as she fumed. He might have the right to deadline the *Tala*, but she was going to have his ass for keeping her out of the loop and embarrassing her in front of the skipper.

"What do you want me to see in here? I don't have a multiscan."

"If it takes two days to do the trickle test and reset, that means your check flight will be in three days," he said quietly.

"So?" she asked, confused by his change in
tack. "What's in three days?" She shrugged.

"Not here. Somewhere else. Like New Cebu."

"The wedding," she said as it all fell into place.

A check flight required passing through at least four Class B or higher gates, but which gates were generally left up to the pilot. Her heart beat faster. She could just "happen" to take her check flight to New Cebu. Once there, she could land the *Tala* and have a ground tech check the readings. Nothing odd about that. Three or four hours there, and she'd have enough time, if everything were coordinated, to be in San Miguel for the ceremony. It wouldn't be the first time a pilot had done that to see a spouse or partner for a quickie, if nothing else.

Then her heart fell again. She couldn't do it. Making a quick stop was one thing. Making it after being denied leave was something else. She appreciated what Josh was doing, but she couldn't put him in that position.

She squeezed his arm and said, "Thank you, Josh, but I can't do it. Too much risk."

"Who do you think told me to check the synch comb? Who told me that it might need a trickle test?"

"What? I don't know . . ."

Except she did. Commander Tuominen. This was his idea. He was a GT, after all, one of the entitled class. He'd approved her leave, and he'd have taken the admiral's disapproval as an affront to his authority. She might be an admiral and he a commander, but he was also a Tuominen, one of the elite families among the elite. She could ruin him as a Navy officer, if she so chose, but among the Golden Tribe, he was much higher on the social ladder.

And all of this explained his last comment, about taking the *Tala* to HTA. There was a direct gate from Refuge to New Cebu, but she'd have to file her initial flight plan, and that could raise a few eyebrows. She could even be grounded before she took off. But going to HTA, which was out of First Fleet's command? She could jump from there to Pyrus, and from that nexus, right to New Cebu. Three jumps and she'd be home.

"So, what do you want me to do? Trickle test? It's your call?" he whispered to her.

A smile broke over her face. This could be military suicide. But even if she was caught, what could they do to her? Shave her head and send her to fight the FALs?

"No use taking any chances, AT3 Frye. Trickle charge her!"

Chapter 12

Beth nervously waited for the dress to print out. She was the only customer in the White Duck, Station 3's lone civilian concession. Retired Lieutenant Commander Tracy Ruiz, the owner of the shop, was behind her desk engrossed in the latest simu-romance on her pad.

The last two days had been nerve-wracking, expecting an alert at any moment. Normally, she wanted to take it to the FALs, eager for any opportunity. She wanted the FALs to pay for Lieutenant Hadley, for Hurl, and Trout. This time, she prayed that the bastards would take a few days off. Her heart dropped when the task force went to Condition Alpha: four crystal ships had appeared within human space, but the VFX51 Scorpions got the call, and the four ships winked back to wherever they came from before the squadron's Wasps could engage. But for once, the capricious gods of war had mercy on her, and Beth woke up bright and early for her check ride.

But there had still been one more thing she had to do. Yesterday, after calling Mercy and telling her she'd make the wedding, but in her flight suit, the bridezilla had put her foot down and demanded that she wear her bridesmaid dress. Due to the circumstances and time constraints, Beth had assumed that popping in wearing her flight suit would be OK, but Mercy was having none of it. So, after briefly considering the ship's store, she boarded one of the early shuttles for Station 3 and was waiting for Tracy when she came to open the shop.

She downloaded the dress specs Mercy had sent along with her sizes, and two minutes later, she had the dress in hand. It was a rather bright shade of orange, a tone that made Beth's skin look sallow, but she tried it on, hoping it would look better than she feared.

It didn't.

Beth stared at her reflection in horror.

"Tracy," she called out hopefully from the mirror in front of the dressing room. "Did this print out correctly?"

"You uploaded it, not me," Tracey said, not bothering to look up from her pad.

She knew it printed correctly, though. It fit perfectly, and she was assuredly the smallest person on the station. The bright orange strapless gown hugged her torso tight, then ballooned into a ball around her waist, hips, and thighs.

"I swear to God, Mercy. I know the bridesmaids should never outshine the bride, but this? I look like a friggin' pumpkin."

Beth wasn't a fashion whore, but this . . . this was pretty bad. She hadn't bothered to look at the design when a happy Mercy had sent her the specs. Now, she was doubly glad she hadn't used the kiosk on the *Victory*, taking the shuttle to Station 3 and the White Duck instead. Something this . . . *unique* would have garnered unwanted attention.

And now it was too late to do anything about it. She should have insisted that she wear her uniform.

No, that was never going to pass muster.

She should have printed out her dress two days ago, then made some minor mods to make it look less . . . like it looked now. She looked at her watch. It was 0848 in San Miguel, and there was no time to do anything about the dress. She had about two hours to make it back to the ship, register with Flight Ops, and then launch and fly through each gate and to New Cebu and San Miguel in time for the wedding.

She rolled her eyes and shrugged out of the dress, rolling it up and stuffing it in her flight pack, along with a pair of white flats. The pack barely closed.

"Thanks, Tracy," she shouted out as she affirmed payment and bolted from the store. "See you next time."

With the squadron deployed and the SEALs who-knew where, the main station was eerily quiet. It wasn't until she approached the hangar that the hustle and bustle took back over. With the station's surfeit of industrial printers, the

Victory's maintenance and engineering staff were making use of them while they could. Good for Beth, though. With the traffic between the two, there was a ship's shuttle leaving almost every hour.

She made it with ten minutes to spare. No one gave her a second look as she boarded the shuttle. Her trip to the station was being logged, of course, but it was her home station, after all, and no one would think twice about it.

She hoped.

Twenty-three minutes after launch, the shuttle eased into Delta Hangar. She was doing fine with time, so she held back while five yellowshirts horsed a big hunk of featureless metal— Beth didn't have a clue as to what it was for—onto a mule and then off the shuttle. Clutching her pack, she went back to the squadron spaces and into her small stateroom. Normally, a mere second class petty officer would be in open berthing, but the pilots were all kept together, and with Mercy now on convalescent leave, she had the space to herself.

She shucked her pilot blues, and jumped in the sonic for a quick shower, remembering to give her body a double spray of antibac. She wouldn't have time to clean up once she reached home, and she didn't want to stink up the ceremony. She grimaced as the stringent spray burned her nasal passages. Usually, with just her in the cockpit, she was content to stink it up.

"What I do for you, sista," she muttered.

She checked her watch. She could have filed her flight plan any time after Joshua started the reset, but she wanted as little attention put on her as possible, and doing it early gave the ops staff just that much more time to take issue with her initial destination. It wasn't as if using HTA was verbotten, but someone might get a hair up their ass and insist that she use First Fleet's Corozon Training Area.

"Josh, is she ready?" she called her plane captain and asked, unable to simply sit and do nothing.

"Of course," he said. "I did the final checks an hour ago. Everything looks good."

This might be one huge con job, but the reset was a reality, and Josh's first priority was to make sure the *Tala* was combat operational. It probably killed him to have the fighter down for two days, as if it was an affront to his maintenance skills.

Beth realized this was a pretty big sacrifice for him, and she owed him.

She sat on the edge of her rack and waited, watching the time tick down ever-so-slowly. Finally, eight minutes earlier than she promised herself, she left her stateroom and made her way to flight ops, sure that everyone she passed could see the guilt plastered over her face.

"Petty Officer Dalisay," a voice called out behind her just as she reached Flight Ops, making her jump.

"Yes, sir?" she asked Commander Tuominen, her voice cracking.

"I saw on the POD that you were taking your Wasp out on its check flight?"

"Yes, sir. I'm about to register it now."

"Make sure you get her back online. I don't like having any of our fighters deadlined."

"Aye, aye, sir," she squeaked out.

"And let's make sure this is an uneventful check-ride, OK?" he said quietly, but with a forceful tone that left no doubt that he was really saying, "Don't make me regret this." "Aye-aye, sir," she said again.

He looked at her for a long moment before turning around and going back the way he'd come. Beth took in a long breath, then entered Flight Ops.

Filing her flight plan was something of an anticlimax. PO1 Addab didn't even look up as she entered the initial destination and the details appeared on the Flight Board in the back of the space. Beth hesitated a moment, waiting for the *j'accuse*, but no one said a word.

Just get on with it, she had to tell herself. *Act normally.*

Next stop was the ready room locker. It was empty, which was fine with her. She got into her flight suit, grabbed her flight pack, and then went out to Josh and the *Tala*. Her nerves wanted to scream as she did her pre-flight check, Josh calmly following her as if everything was routine.

But it wasn't routine. Going into combat, Beth was excited to be flying. There was a tinge of fear, but that only served to hype her up more. This time, fear was taking over her. She almost decided not to go through with it. She still had to do the check flight, but she'd just skip the wedding. No harm, no foul.

No harm? Mercy will never forgive me.

The 15-minute pre-flight finally finished, and Beth boarded her Wasp, her flight pack safely tucked inside the knee panel. As a yellowshirt tractored her over to the launch rail, she started to relax. That is, until she saw the Command Master Chief standing with Josh on the observer rail. Josh didn't look happy.

She kept craning her neck to watch them as the Tala settled on the rail, sure that Chief Orinoco knew what she'd planned. She expected to be shut down any minute. The chief was frowning as she watched, but then again, that was her normal visage.

Finally, the cat officer came on her comms with, "Foxtrotsix-mike-zero one-niner, are you green for launch?"

"Roger, green, CAT."

"Understand green. Standby, launch in five . . . four . . ."

Beth waited for the "Scratch launch, sure that it was coming as she mimed kissing her cross, but the countdown continued.

". . . three . . . two . . . one . . . launch."

Beth's head snapped back as the Tala shot down the rails and out into the black. She was out of the ship, but she didn't relax until release of control and the *Tala's* engine kicked in. She was on her way.

****

Four hours, thirty-six minutes later, the Tala popped through the Rizal Gate and into the New Cebu system. She'd filed this leg of her flight two minutes before entering the gate, and even then, she half-expected someone to notice and give her orders to abort and return to the *Victory*. She could still get those orders now, but with the orange and brown planet looming large on her cockpit display, she felt like she was home.

She looked at her comms link, tempted to turn it off, a victim of a technical glitch. But there was a war going on, and she couldn't go that far. She could make use of it, though.

"Mercy, I'm in-system," she told her friend after patching through the Navy hub in orbit over the planet.

"Thank God, Beth. I was afraid you were going to miss the ceremony. We're still on for twenty-three hundred."

With forces scattered around the galaxy, the Navy still used GMT from back on Earth. That made local time a moving target due to different planetary rotational rates, but at the present, that made the wedding in the early afternoon, just over two hours from now.

"I'll be there."

She'd be cutting it close, however. She still had to land at the dual civilian/Navy Reserve spaceport at White Mountain, turn the Wasp over for a quick analysis (her excuse for landing), and catch a hop to San Miguel.

"How are you feeling? Excited? You look beautiful," Beth added, taking in the sight of her best friend in her wedding gown. As bad as the bridesmaids' dresses were, Mercy's formfitting, high-collared wedding dress was stunning.

"Thanks. Thank God for your mother, though, taking care of everything. I could never have pulled this off on my own. Speaking of looking beautiful, do you have your dress? Where is it?" she asked, craning her head as if that would let her see more through the cam.

"Right here," Beth said, pulling out the pack.

"Do you like it? Does it fit?"

"It fits," Beth said, leaving it at that. "How do you feel? Excited?" she asked, changing the subject.

"Nervous as shit," Mercy said. "I hope we're doing the right thing."

Beth kept the grin plastered on her face. She'd come to terms, even welcomed Mercy and Rocky's relationship, but she thought the wedding was premature, one brought on by the contingencies of war. Now was not the time, however, to voice that opinion.

"You two love each other. That's what matters. But I've got to cut this short. I need to report in to traffic control. See you in a couple of hours."

"Two hours," Mercy said. "Two, not a couple."

"Relax. That's what 'a couple' means. I'll make it."

And she should make it. New Cebu only had the Rizal gate, and there was nothing else in the system of note. Even with the gate comparatively close to the planet, a commercial liner might take three hours to get into orbit, then debark passengers by shuttle to the surface. But Beth was in a Wasp, which could approach the planet at a much higher rate of speed, then land itself. No need for a shuttle.

"You better, sista," Mercy said. "I need my maid of honor here."

New Cebu traffic control would have seen her come through the gate, and as a Navy vessel, she was not required to check in. This was a routine flight, however, so it was good form to let them know she was coming in. They gave her an inbound route, all the way to the White Mountain spaceport. Usually, she'd accept the handshake, turning over the control of the *Tala* to them, but they'd bring her in at commercial ship speed, which would get her there too late. Luckily, she was navy, and she didn't have to rely on them. She was straddling a comet, after all, not a donkey cart.

"That's a negative, NC Control. I think I'll take her in myself."

"Don't blame you, Navy Foxtrot-six-mike-zero one-niner. You've got yourself some ride there, but we've got intervening traffic. You're going to have to hold up before entering Papa-Lima airspace."

"NC Control, do I have to remind you I only checked in as a courtesy?"

"And we appreciate that. But we've got a Papa-Victor launch at White Mountain. It won't be clear for 70 minutes."

Beth shook her head. A Papa-Victor launch gave civilian ports a case of the jitters. Just last year, a Papa-Victor blew up on Hari. Over a hundred people were killed, and the spaceport was shut down for three months before the decon teams cleared it to reopen.

Navy pilots handled much more dangerous cargo on a daily basis, so they tended to look down upon the more conservative civilian staffs.

She checked the time. Her ETA at *Tala's* 80% specs was 43 minutes. If she closed the gap, but then waited above the reentry envelope until White Mountain was reopened for traffic, she could land in 84 minutes. That would be cutting it close, but it was still doable. What she didn't need was to barge her way in, then have the local authorities submit a formal protest that would catch the notice of her command.

And if worse came to worst, she could bypass White Mountain. She was in a military fighter, after all, and she could land anywhere. It would probably raise more questions, and negate her supposed reason for landing at White Mountain, but she hadn't come this far just to miss the wedding. She could fly to the RE point, give her self a drop-dead time, and shift to San Miguel's helo pad if she hit that. She quickly looked up the coordinates for the pad, then entered it in the system . . . just in case.

"Understand, NC Control. I'll wait at the RE point for your clearance."

"Thanks, Navy," the man on the other side said with evident relief. "I'll keep you updated."

She checked the time again. It was going to be tight if she was going to land at White Mountain. Mercy had hired a maglev to take her to San Miguel, but the rentals were programmed at set speeds. With the delay, she'd be arriving just as the ceremony was getting started. No time to shower and change.

She looked down at the flight pack. She could save time by changing now. It wasn't as if she was going to be putting the *Tala* through her paces to where she'd need the support her flight suit or helmet offered.

Beth could change in the maglev as well, but the rental agencies monitored the cab interiors, and she wasn't keen on the idea of changing while others watched.

"Oh, hell. Might as well do it."

She popped the seal and took off the neck-cracker, then released her flight suit seam and started wiggling out of it, which was no mean feat. Wasp cockpits were cramped, and most pilots wouldn't have been able to shuck their suits. Luckily, Beth was small, so what might have been impossible for others was merely difficult for her. After almost dislocating her shoulder in a move that would make a circus contortionist proud, she had her flight suit off and shoved to the firewall at her feet.

Without the flight suit's temperature controls, her butt felt cold on her seat. There were always rumors of pilots taking holos of themselves naked while their ships were deep in the black, but that wasn't going to happen with her. She didn't feel naughty—just cold. Goosebumps rose on her arms.

Her comms light flashed on, and she jumped. Without her helmet, she couldn't accept the call, and she hadn't yet switched it over to normal cockpit control. She started to give the order before she slapped her hand over her mouth. She didn't know who was trying to reach her yet, but she couldn't do it like this. She pinched the flight suit between her toes and pulled it up until she could grab it, then with the back seam open, slid her arms into the sleeves. Her back was bare, and the body of the suit was simply draped on top of her lap like an apron, but her upper torso should look like she was dressed. At least she hoped so.

"Revert to cockpit display," she ordered.

Immediately, Master Chief Orinoco's face looked out at her from the comms screen, and her heart fell.

"It's about time, Dalisay. What took you so long . . . and where's your helmet?"

"I took it off," she answered, stating the obvious.

"Those helmets were issued to save lives, but they can't do anything unless you wear them."

"I'm in-system, Master Chief, away from the war zone."

"Everywhere's a war zone, Dalisay, or didn't you hear about the incursion yesterday? But forget about that for now. Where are you?"

For a brief moment, she was tempted to lie. But that was stupid. Orinoco knew where she was. Beth had just filed her flight plan.

"I just came through the Rizal Gate," she said, unwilling to just say she was approaching New Cebu. Orinoco was going to have to pry it out of her.

"And where are you headed, on your *check flight*?" When Beth said nothing, she asked, "You're not heading down to New Cebu now, right? Not when your leave was disapproved?"

"Check flights are left to the discretion of the pilots, Master Chief. I can go wherever I want."

Beth was in the wrong, even if not technically, and Orinoco was in the right, but she was not going to admit it. She was going to cling to the technicality and let things fall out as they may after her return.

"And you filed for HTA."

"I filed for Pyrus and New Cebu, too. I need four gate jumps before the *Tala* can be cleared for combat ops."

"Two minutes. You filed for New Cebu two minutes before the jump," the command master chief said accusingly.

"There's no time requirement. I filed before I jumped."

"If you think I believe that stinking pile of shit, you're stupider than I thought. You're disobeying the orders of the admiral, missy, and you're going to pay the price. And don't think you can bat your eyes at the CO and worm your way out of trouble. Even he's going to have to admit his pet NEP went over the line."

Beth stared at her in shock. First, that the chief was insinuating that she would try and flirt with the CO. Second, that the CO held her in any different regard from the other pilots.

Her gaze hardened as anger took over. She had to control her voice when she said, "Command Master Chief Orinoco, at the moment, I am on an operational mission. If you have a problem with it, please bring it up with the commanding officer.
Otherwise, if there is nothing else, I'm cutting the link."

The command master chief was a powerful woman, and she had a lot of control over Beth and the other enlisted pilots. What she didn't have was any operational authority over the pilots. Even the NEPs. Beth was lighting a fire under the chief, and she'd pay the price after she got back, but for the moment, the woman had no authority over her.

Lightning almost flew from the chief's eyes, but she bit back the eruption that Beth could see roiling under the surface, and calmly said, "Very well, Petty Officer Second Class Dalisay. You complete your mission. Then, after you've returned, after you've closed the log, I'd like to see you in my office.
Understood?"

"Sure thing, Command Master Chief. See you then," Beth said, then cut off the comms.

She sat statue-still for a moment, then slammed her hand against her display. "FUCK!" She was steaming angry.

How dare she?

That crack about batting her eyes was too much. Beth was too professional for that, and not only because the CO was a commander and she was a petty officer. Intimate relations between the two was not tolerated. But he was also a GT, one of the Golden Tribe. Both norms and GTs were human, and there were the occasional hook-ups between them, but it was far rarer than the holovids might lead people to believe.

Still fuming, Beth unhooked the neck seam of her flight suit and let it fall back to the deck at her feet again. Her sour mood didn't help as she shook out the monstrosity of a bridesmaid's dress, then, wriggling like an inch-worm in acid, slipped into it. The horrible puffy spherical section was scrunched in the close confines of her seat, temporarily giving it the appearance of close to a normal-looking dress. If it was wrinkled when she got out, well, screw it, and Mercy better not say a word if she wanted to live through the ceremony.

She folded her arms across her chest and settled in for the rest of the approach.

****

Beth was still in a funk thirty-five minutes later, New Cebu huge in her display, when "Navy Foxtrot-six-mike-zero one-niner, this is New Cebu Control," broke the silence in the cockpit.

Shit. Here it is, she thought, as her heart sunk.

Orinoco must have gone to someone who did have authority over her flight, probably either the commander or the duty "FOO," the Flight Operations Officer. She was going to get orders to abort her flight and return to the *Victory.*

I shouldn't have pissed the asshole off.

But what was done was done. "This is Navy fighter Six-sixmike-zero one-niner on a check flight. What do you have for me?" she asked, trying sound innocent.

"Maybe nothing, Navy. We've just had some strange readings for the last half-hour, and we can't make heads nor tails of it. But with you in-system, the director thought that since you're Navy, maybe you've seen this before or have better scanners."

Her heart skipped a beat, and a sense of foreboding swept over her. The guy hadn't given her much, but still . . .

"Give me the coordinates, New Cebu. I'll check it out."

The coordinates were there almost before the words were out of her mouth.

"*Tala*, full sensor array," she ordered, then sat there biting her lip as the systems came online.

The *Tala* had been on routine status with only nav, gate synch, and comms online. She wasn't on a combat mission, after all, and the ops sec folk liked to minimize the more powerful emissions when they weren't needed.

It took about thirty seconds for the *Tala* to be completely operational. Beth inputted the coordinates and went right to the TSM-4, the main scanner array. She saw what was bothering them on the Kilting band. Nothing concrete, but a definite flux in the wave, something that shouldn't be there . . . and something heading straight to New Cebu, like a bow-wave of a torpedo closing in on a wet-water ship. The torpedo might not be visible, the bow-wave sure was.

Not one. Two, she realized.

This was exactly what they'd seen at Niue, and before they'd figured it out, they'd lost four fighters. That was a quarter of the galaxy away, deep into the center, but she knew in her heart that the two anomalies were FALs and their crystal ships.

"New Cebu Control, go to General Emergency Condition Alpha!" she shouted over the comms as she entered a new course to bypass the planet and intercept the approaching ships. "And contact the Navy Command Center, give them my ship designator, my current heading, and tell them two crystal ships have appeared in system."

"Crystals? The aliens? That's impossible. They're on the other side of the galaxy," the comms operator said.

"'Impossible or not,' she told him, 'They're on their freaking way to you right now. Just do what I told you!"

Fear knotted her gut. She didn't know if the crystals were on an attack run or not. There were civilian ships in the area, easy targets. But they could be on a recce mission; hell, they could be FAL tourists, if that even existed. Something told Beth, however, that this was an attack, and not on some commercial liners. The ghost bow-wave was heading towards the planet. Without any defenses, New Cebu could be devastated by even two of their fighters—and her family was down there.

But the planet did have a defense. Her. She had to stop the FALs.

She armed the *Tala*, and almost as an afterthought, turned on the new clone projector. She didn't even know if the thing worked yet. It was just one more gadget Jean Luc had added to the rest, and it wouldn't be the first new system that his R&D team developed that was rushed into service and ended up being useless. But on her own facing at least two FALs, she needed every advantage she could get.

"Connect to Commander Tuominen," she ordered. She had to report in, no matter what happened. She couldn't trust the civilian Traffic Control to do it without going through all the steps up their reporting chain, and that could be too late. She should report it through the FOO, but she didn't know who was on duty, and she didn't want to go through an explanation. The commander could cut through all the bullshit.

"Commander Tuominen, this is Petty Officer Dalisay--"

"I know who you are, Dalisay," he said as his image came onto her display. His eyes widened ever-so-slightly as he took in her in the dress. "What do you want?"

"I've got two FALs, sir, heading in to New Cebu. I told Traffic Control to report the contact to the Navy, but you know civilians. It might take a while."

"FALs? The Command Master Chief was just in my office, demanding that I recall you to the *Victory* to face mast. Is this some sort of BS game you've concocted? If it is, you've gone too far. I was going to wait, but with this—"

"Pull up my telemetries," she told him as she started running fire-control solutions for her three weapon systems. "Check my TSM-4."

Beth knew she was going to have to engage the FALs, and she had three choices, at this point. She didn't even consider the L-20 laser, which had so far proven to be about worthless against the crystal ships. She had her G-21 railgun, and she'd gotten two of her four kills with it, but that was an anomaly. The railgun was only for close-in fighting, atmospheric air-to-air, or ground support. The rounds, even at hypervelocity speeds were just too slow. Fire too early, and even a mining barge could dodge out of the way.

That left two choices, her M-57 torpedoes or her P-13 Hadron Coil Particle Beam. She ran the options through her mind. Of the two, the P-13 was a light-speed weapon, but it took a while to knock out a crystal ship, and the longer it was fired, radiation and heat buildup in the Wasp became problematic. The torpedoes locked onto and chased their targets, and if they hit, they could knock any ship out, FAL or human. Getting them to hit, however, was the problem."

The commander came back and said, 'Try to divert the FALs. If not, engage. Keep them off the planet. We'll have three flights there in three hours, and I've already set the alert with

HQ. If they have anything closer, I'll let you know."

"Aye-aye, sir. Understand."

And she did understand. At interstellar distances, a battle might barely advance over three hours, but this was in-system. Three hours was a long time, and whatever was going to happen would have happened by then. All she could hope for was to beat the two crystals, or if they were going to splash her, divert them away from the planet long enough for the cavalry to arrive.

For a moment, she considered getting back into her flight suit, but she dismissed the notion out of hand. It had been almost impossible to get out of the suit inside the *Tala's* cockpit, and getting back in would be even worse, and she didn't have Josh there to make the connections. Better not to risk getting tangled up. Besides, looking at her battle comp display, even at slower in-system speeds, she could beat them around the planet and intercept them at the speeds the *Tala's* compensators could handle.

She ran two simulations, one with the torps and one with the P-13, hoping for a clear choice, but neither resulted in a high POS. She was going to have to see how things progressed.

And, of course, as they were wont to do, the crystals changed the picture. Beth was still one-point-eight million klicks from the planet when the FALs upped the ante. If she had hoped they might be a recce flight, they dispelled that notion when they fired one of their round torpedoes, not at her, but at the planet. The torp was immediately visible as it exited whatever hid the crystal ships, and it was a big one, bigger than any she'd seen before. The mass and speed alone could make this an extinction event, like with the dinosaurs on Earth. But those were her family and friends down there, not dinosaurs. Beth was not going to let that damned thing reach the planet.

Without thinking, Beth hit G-Shot and increased her speed. She was below the orbital plane, while the FALs were above it, and she had to close the distance if she wanted her torps to have a shot at diverting the thing—which she now knew she had to use. The decision had been made for her. She might be able to disable the FAL torpedo with her P-13, but the hulking thing would still continue on its trajectory, and even a dead lump of crystal torpedo would cause a tremendous amount of damage on the planet if it hit.

She immediately regretted changing into the dress. Even with a flight suit, G-Shot burned like acid as it flowed into her body to allow her to stand more force. Without the suit, even her skin was on fire.

The *Tala* jumped forward like a racehorse, and combined with the FAL's speed, the distance closed. Beth's comms lit up from the panicked Traffic Control. They'd have seen the torpedo as well, but with the G-Shot taking over, she didn't have the time nor inclination to calm them down. She had to focus. "Keep running the firing solutions," she ordered the *Tala*.

Beth would never get a 100% Probability of Success, so she had to take her best shot. The graph kept changing as more data poured in, but it looked like her best would be seventy-two percent. Good, but when she was dealing with five-hundred million souls on the planet, that wasn't good enough. She locked in targeting for all three of her torps, but then she wondered if the FALs had another of them. There were two crystal ships, after all. She had to keep back one of the torps for that possibility.

Her first alarm went off. The *Tala* was under fire from a FAL beam projector. The eggheads were still not sure exactly how they worked, but they were deadly. Somehow, they found the molecular resonance of a Wasp's shields, then the outer skin and set up a resonating frequency that vibrated the molecules, building up heat until the fighter came apart. Cooked. The *Tala* had a latticed polycarbon web surrounding the hull in hopes that it would slow down the resonance. It hadn't helped Mercy on her last mission, though.

"Or maybe it did. She lost her fighter, but she survived," Beth muttered to herself. "That and the neck-cracker."

She glanced at her own neck-cracker, still beside her. With a sigh, she put it on. Without her suit on, it didn't seal, but it was powered up. It took her a moment to adjust to the display.

It looked like only one of the crystal ships was firing at her, but it was enough. In only ten seconds, the *Tala's* shields were down to eighty-eight percent.

Even with her brain fuzzy from G-Shot, she knew she had to fire. Her torps did not have the same shielding as the *Tala* had, and they could not survive long under the FALs beam weapon. She'd already programmed a divergent approach, coming in on the FAL torp from different directions. The probability of a kill hit sixty-four percent, but started dropping as her combat AI considered the enemy projector. She couldn't wait any longer.

"Fire one and two!" she shouted before turning in and up to the two FALs. With the combined closing rate of the three torpedoes, two of hers and one of theirs, Beth would know in thirty-three seconds if she'd taken it out.

Immediately, the FAL projector shifted from the *Tala* to one of the torps. Beth had to keep their attention on her. She still had one torp and her hadron cannon. Not being able to pinpoint the crystal ship, she targeted the torp on where the bow-wave indicated one of them was, then opened fire with her cannon on where she thought the other one was.

She was approaching her G-Shot time limits, but she couldn't afford to cut it off now. She was going to have to take evasive action, and she couldn't handicap the *Tala* with her body's inability to handle high Gs.

But for the moment, Beth was stuck in her approach. With the dogfights against the FALs so far, the winner was generally the one whose shields could outlast the other's. Pilots in their Wasps could maneuver to break contact for a moment, but the effects were cumulative. Now, against the two FALs, she couldn't break contact. She had to bear in, to make them break contact. A big game of chicken, to see who'd blink.

The enemy fighter didn't blink. Beth's cannon beam disrupted its scan shielding enough that it failed, and suddenly two crystal ships popped up on her display. The one firing looked like a standard crystal fighter. The second one, the one that had fired the torpedo, was twice the size. Beth didn't know what that indicated, nor did she have time to contemplate that. She had to disrupt the smaller one, and with them now visible, she could focus her beam tighter, to put more energy on the target in hopes of burning through. There was no maneuvering now, just three ships closing in on each other."

It was the smaller FAL fighter's weapon that drew first blood. At nineteen seconds to impact, Beth's first torp was knocked out. She had one left to take out the FAL torp, and she regretted only firing two. She was already past the perpendicular to the enemy torpedo, and while she could spin on her axis and fire the third one, instead of closing, it would be chasing, and with the two FALs much closer to it.

She had to stop the crystal ship that was firing. If that FAL torpedo got through to the planet, Beth didn't want to imagine how many lives would be lost. She switched to target her third M-57 torpedo at the smaller crystal ship and fired. The *Tala* was already at point-seven-two-C, and her torp had a good lock. As it shot ahead, it would reach the FAL crystal in ten seconds— but would it be soon enough? She came close to redlining her cannon as she poured power into it, and her radiation and temperature levels were climbing dangerously.

She had to take care of her temps. Her radiators couldn't keep up, so she started ejecting fireturds, the molypendium billets, which after they were heated to the molten state by the *Tala*'s heat buildup, were fired into the cold reaches of space. Ejecting them created a small warp in her shielding that could be exploited, but overheating would take her out of the fight the same as getting a crystal torp up her ass.

Beth's mind was getting fuzzy around the edges from the GShot and acceleration, but she was latched to the first torp's telemetry. Its little shield started to fail just as her third torp hit the FAL ship. The pilot had played chicken and lost.

Beth shifted her course to cut off the bigger ship when her first torpedo hit the planet killer, exploding it into its component atoms. Part of her, the still sane part, wanted to cheer, but it took all her effort to focus on the second ship. Her brain felt like it was in a bag full of cotton, and she wanted to sink into its embrace of oblivion.

"'No, Floribeth! Not yet!' she had to scream.

She told the *Tala* to target the ship with the beamer, then to max the acceleration to close the distance. She didn't know how long she could stand it. She had taken the G-Shot, but she was in the pumpkin dress, not her flight suit. Normally, maybe three minutes. Now . . . ?

But she was closing the distance between the two fighters. She had vague, fuzzy thoughts about ramming it, but the numbers were wrong. If it remained on its course, she could get within forty-two-thousand klicks, a stone's throw by interstellar standards, but not near close enough to ram. She had to keep pouring hadron beam into it and hope for the best.

The *Tala* shuddered, and alarms blared. Beth couldn't concentrate, and it took her a moment to realize her P-13 cannon had been knocked out. The *Tala* started bleeding acceleration, alarms blaring for her attention. Her hand automatically reached up to check her helmet seal before she remembered that her neck-cracker was just sitting on her head, not sealed. and that struck her as funny. She started cackling like a mad woman until a blip appeared in front of the FAL ship and started to accelerate. Death on the way. That shocked her sober, the cotton mind gone.

The second enemy torp was almost a million klicks away and separating. The *Tala* was at point-seven-three-C. All Beth had was her G-21 railgun, which fired depleted uranium rounds at five-thousand meters per second. Consider the FAL torpedo's speed, add on the Tala's speed, and that was threehundred-thousand meters times point-seven-three and an oblique of . . . hell, even with a clear mind, she didn't have the math for that, and she couldn't mumble out the commands clear enough for the targeting computer to do the calculations.

The railgun was fixed in place and was aimed by spinning the entire fighter around. The ship would keep traveling on its previous course, but the prow—and railgun—would now be aiming at the target. With shaky hands, she switched the targeting system to manual, spun the *Tala* around, and using the crosshairs and more then a bit of Kentucky windage, fired off three long belts of ammo, sending six-hundred quarterkilogram inert rounds at the enemy torpedo as it started to accelerate to New Cebu, which was hanging large in the black of space.

The gods of war are a capricious lot, and they loved nothing better than to screw up the strategic experts who have a plan for every contingency. Sometimes, they also love to reward the stupid and unprepared. Beth figured she must have been their quota for that second category. Somehow, against all odds, one of those 600 rounds hit the enemy torp as it sped off. Even a quarter-kilo traveling at those speeds is deadly. The torpedo came apart into a million pieces. They'd still reach the planet, but most would burn up in entry, giving the people a nice show.

But there was still the last FAL ship. Beth didn't know how many torpedoes it carried. The *Tala's* alarms went off again, this time from the FAL projector. The *Tala's* shields were down to thirty-four-point-one and dropping. She really didn't care about that. All she could think about was the enemy ship. The two ships, one human, one FAL, would be at their closest point in about ten seconds.

Beth could have . . . *should* have . . . told the *Tala* to target the enemy ship, but by then, her mind was barely functioning. All she could think of was to kill it. She spun the *Tala* around, zooming in the railgun's targeting scope, and targeted it. At forty-thousand-whatever kilometers, even on manual with the targeting assist, she couldn't miss. Beth started firing, emptying the last twelve-hundred rounds. The FAL ship seemed to realize what was going on, but too late. It began to move to the side when the first rounds slammed into it, and that's all she wrote.

Beth was numb, and not just from the G-Shot. She'd somehow managed to shoot down two FAL torpedoes and two ships. It just didn't register. With her laser focus on the enemy broken, her mind slowed to a stop. There was still something she had to do, something important, but she couldn't quite place it. The *Tala's* alarms were blaring for her attention, almost burrowing into her brain. She jerked off the neckcracker, banging it against the inside of the canopy where it bounced back and hit the side of her head.

As if slapped across the face, Beth had a tiny moment of lucidity. The *Tala* was damaged, and she needed help. Without knowing what was wrong with the fighter, she had to get the Wasp on the ground. She mumbled out the order, knowing she was in no shape to try and fly the *Tala* herself.

The main warning cut off, but that only revealed pulsating alarm, and it took a moment for her to place it. G-Shot. She was well into the warning zone. She gave the order to cut it off, and the tiny nano-pumps started evacuating it from her system. The shock of losing the boost was too much for her abused body, and blackness swept over her.

Jonathan P. Brazee

****

"Satan's balls, sista. Where the hell have you been?"

With an extreme effort of will, Beth managed to pry her eyelids open. A blur, one of three, slowly coalesced into Mercy, still in her wedding dress.

"I . . . FALs, in system. Attacking New Cebu. I got them," she mumbled.

The look of concern on Mercy's face changed as her warrior face took over.

"Fucking FALs? Here? In New Cebu?"

"That's redundant, Mercy. 'Fucking FALs. Fucking Fucking Alien Lifeforms," she said with a giggle.

"Oh, damn it. She's out of it. Probably G-Shot," Mercy said, then added, "Rocky, you and Joseph, get her out of here. And be careful. Sit her on the ground and get her something to drink."

A moment later, hands grabbed her around the shoulders and pulled her out of the *Tala* while Mercy, wedding dress and all, leaned into the cockpit, ass and legs hanging out. Beth could hear her code into the Tala's interface. As a pilot, she wouldn't have the same privileges as Josh or another tech would, but she could access anything operational.

Beth was eased to the ground, and her mother appeared in front of her with a glass of *melon*, holding it to her mouth. Beth took a small swallow, the cold liquid feeling wonderful sliding down her G-Shot-parched throat. She reached up and grabbed the glass, tilting it to drink more.

The cold drink, made by soaking grated cantaloupe in water and sugar, knocked some sense back into her. She looked around. At least twenty people, all dressed in their Sunday finest, were standing, looking at her with concerned eyes. It took her another moment to realize where she was. She'd given the order for the *Tala* to land, but the last coordinates she'd entered were for San Miguel, not White Mountain.

Mercy leaned back, a look of concern on her face. "Holy shit, sista. I think you saved our asses."

"What do you mean, Mercy? What's going on?" Father Jeffrey asked. "Is something wrong."

"Not anymore, Father, thanks to Beth there."

"Sorry I missed your wedding, Mercy," Beth said.

"You haven't missed anything. We delayed it because we didn't know where you were. You were on your way, but then you weren't, and I couldn't raise you. We were worried sick. But never in a million years did I think . . ." she started before looking out at the gathered people. "But never mind about that. We need to get you to the hospital. Does anyone know what happened? I mean from the squadron?"

"The CO knows, and he sent three flights. I don't know what time it is now."

"Let me report in and find out," Mercy said before climbing back into the *Tala's* cockpit and opening up the comms.

Beth leaned back, happy to be letting someone else take over. She was tired, dead tired, and every muscle fiber ached, but her mind was clearing up. She knew she would need two weeks of intensive recuperation to overcome the side effects of the G-Shot, but for the moment, she felt much better than she had any right to feel. Maybe saving a world had something to do with that.

Pretty pretentious of you, Floribeth, she thought, looking at her townspeople, her mother, Rocky. Still, she felt good. No, *great*. She had so closely come to losing those she loved.

"Hey, the CO took the three flights himself. He's leaving two on station and will land the third here. ETA in fifty-seven minutes," Mercy said from the cockpit.

She climbed out of the *Tala* and flopped down beside Beth, wrapping her arms around her.

"I don't know what to say. I mean . . ." she whispered into Beth's ear.

Beth hugged her back, but said nothing.

"I'd never have forgiven myself if you got yourself killed on my wedding day, Beth."

"You know me. I'm tougher than that. Besides, it's not your wedding day yet."

"Don't worry about that. Now, we've got to get you taken care of."

Beth looked up at those still waiting. A couple hundred meters off, the sounds of music reached her, carried by the breeze.

"We've got an hour,"

"What do you mean?" Mercy asked

"Jeeze you can be dense sometimes, Mercy. And I'm the one who's brain is muddled from the G-Shot.

"Rocky, are the guests still gathered at the church?" she asked her brother.

"Most of them. Some are in the square drinking. Some are here," Rocky said, waving a hand at the people standing around them.

"Well, I'd think it is obvious, my sista dear. I don't think I'm up to a walk to the church, so if you want me to be your maid of honor, you'd better get everyone here, and within the next hour. If you don't mind not using the church, that is."

There was dead silence for a moment before Beth's mother went into overdrive, running around like a chicken with its head cut off to get everyone moving. Her son was getting married, and her oldest daughter only had an hour to attend. Nothing was going to get in her way. Beth drifted in and out a bit, but fifteen minutes later, the entire village was gathered around the *Tala* for the ceremony."

The priest started his normal spiel. all about love and devotion to God, each other, and family, when Beth's mother interrupted with, "Sorry Father, but can we get to the good parts? Time's a'wasting."

Father Jeffrey rushed through the ceremony to the "I do's," while Beth stood watching in a daze. She wasn't sure how much of that was from the G-Shot and how much because her little brother and best friend were getting married. But she joined her mother and sisters with tears running down her cheeks as Mercy and Rocky kissed.

The wedding party barely had time to congratulate the new couple and pose for pictures in front of the *Tala* before Commander Tuominen and three others landed adjacent to the helo pad.

Naval Hospital, Refuge

Chapter 13

"So, she's still our command master chief?" Beth asked.

"I think the CO thought it would be better. You know, keep her quiet," Capgun answered. "And she was told that she'd better play ball, or she'd be transferred to some airless moon in the ass-end of the galaxy."

Beth had been at the hospital for eight days now, eight long days. She was feeling better, and she was anxious to get back to the ship. There was no real reason that she had to recuperate on the planet. The *Victory* had very good medical facilities. But the CO had thought it better that she stay out of sight as certain . . . *irregularities* . . . were addressed.

In view of the very public manner in what had happened, the decision had been made to clean up the circumstances. It wouldn't do to have the Navy's first ace in 200 years, the pilot who'd saved a planet, be subject to a courtmartial. Beth's leave request was being retroactively approved, only the records were being fixed to make it look as if Admiral Nzama had approved it prior to the incident. The wedding holo in front of the Tala was being holoshopped so that Beth was in her flightsuit, looking alert and protective. A small public affairs team was going over every aspect of what happened, fixing what had to be fixed, then preparing a narrative of what the players would say if asked.

The media was clamoring for access to Beth, but that wasn't going to happen until the PA team was done with her, and they were using her medical "condition" as an excuse to keep them at bay for now. Beth hated being kept confined to her hospital room, but she was grateful that she was not going to be fed to the wolves without back-up. A Marine M-77 rifle would be her best defense, but a seasoned PA team would do.

Command Master Chief Orinoco had balked at the script being written, threatening to go to the press herself. There had evidently been a shouting match between her and the CO, but in the end, she had come around. Beth had no doubt that she had been threatened. The woman would love to pull Beth down, so the threat had to have been pretty serious. Capgun's theory was as good as anyone's.

"I just need to get back," she told Capgun. "The *Victory* could get orders to deploy any minute now."

"We're not going to deploy in ten minutes. We've still got all those engineers and techs playing Santa's workshop on Sierra Station. If we go, they'll get you to the ship before we leave. 'Sides, I'd be surprised if you weren't pulled off soon."

"What? Why do you say that?" she asked, alarmed.

"You're the first ace in two-hundred years. You saved a planet. The Navy isn't going to want to waste all that good PR. No, you'll get a medal, a big one. And the director himself is going to give it to you, holocams rolling to catch every second of it. Then, a tour while the Navy shows off their newest hero, the poor-girl makes good. Floribeth Salinas O'Shea Dalisay."

"What? Bullshit."

"You know it's true. And it doesn't hurt that you're a hottie."

"Hottie? Are you high?"

Capgun rolled his eyes. "Yeah, I said it. Hot. The newsies are going to eat you up, and the Navy knows it. So, don't expect to be sitting around the *Victory* waiting for the next fight."

Beth frowned. She didn't think it would be as bad as Capgun said, but enough of what he said rang true to give her pause.

"What about you? Or Wingnut? You both have four kills. You'll be aces soon enough."

"But you're the first. And we're both grizzled old farts, not a beautiful young woman with a great backstory. No, me and
Wingnut will be needed on the front lines."

"I'm needed, too."

"Yeah, there is that. But you can do the Navy more good by being out there in the public's eye, encouraging other young boys and girls to join up, by convincing the politicians that the fight can be won. That's where the Navy needs you."
"It isn't going to be that bad," Beth said.

But she had a feeling, a bad one, that he could be right.

FS VICTORY

Chapter 14

"Hey, it's the Pumpkin Ace," the two new scout pilots said as she walked by, both giving her big smiles and thumbs up. "Way to go!"

Beth faltered, gave a half-smile and a weak wave of acknowledgment. First, it was probably the only time any scout pilot had acknowledged her, and second, "Pumpkin Ace?" *What the heck does that mean?*

She shook her head as she turned into the squadron spaces. She'd just arrived back on the ship after being the only passenger on the captain's gig, and the CO had requested that she see him the moment she stepped back onboard. Without any gear but the rumpled uniform on her back (courtesy of Capgun bringing down one of her spares), she'd headed immediately to the hangar to check out the *Tala* and the waiting Josh. Her plane captain had the *Tala* in tip-top shape, even down to the seven kills now emblazoned on the nose: six crystal ships and two torpedoes. She hadn't even realized a torpedo kill counted, but Gollum had told her the brass had given her the credit since they were planet-killers, not normal, anti-ship torps. Almost as an afterthought, and only once he gone over every detail of what he'd done to the *Tala*, Josh mentioned that Commander Tuominen wanted to see her as soon as she returned aboard.

"Nice that you bothered to mention that, Josh," she told him, checking the time.

She'd been aboard for 43 minutes, already. She lifted her arm, gave her pit a sniff, and then shrugged. The skipper didn't specify that she had to be looking all spit and polish.

She decided against stopping at her stateroom for a clean uniform and headed directly to his office.

Beth passed the command master chief's office, but the hatch was closed, so she didn't have to suffer the glares that would surely be coming her way. The CO's office space was open, though, and she knocked on the edge of the hatch.

"Sir, you wanted to see me?"

He looked up and said, "Ah, yes, Petty Officer Dalisay. Come on in. Take a seat."

When he'd shown up at San Miguel, he'd never mentioned his role in her trip. He'd been anxious to get her back and into treatment, and there was the fact that the *Tala* needed work before it would be recertified to fly again. He'd also visited her twice while she was at the hospital, and once again, neither time did he mention his part in her trip to New Cebu. She figured that he hadn't wanted to mention it with all the civilians in her village listening in, and the hospital was little better in keeping secrets. Now, would be the time for him to lay into her, to get their story straight.

But he didn't ask her to close the hatch. She faltered a moment, pointing back at it, but he shook his head and again told her to sit.

"How are you feeling, Dalisay? Are you feeling fully recovered?"

"Yes, sir. I'm fine," she said a little warily.

There's an elephant in the room with us, and he's making small talk?

"The doctors gave you a clean bill of health, but sometimes, there's lingering fatigue from the G-Shot. Or so I've been told. I've never G-Shotted, just that one simulation during flight school."

"No, sir. I'm fine."

"OK, well, I know you want to check out your Wasp. AT3 Frye has been on it, and she's fully operational. Good man, Frye."

"Yes, he is, sir," she said, wondering where the conversation was going. She knew the *Tala* was ready.

Joshua had been down on the planet to see her four times since he'd gotten the fighter back into shape.

"I imagine you're ready for operations, right?" he asked, but before she could answer, he said, "But I'm afraid that's going to have to be put on the back burner for now."

What? Did Orinoco manage to get me off flight status? she wondered half-rising out of her seat.

"You and I are going to be taking a little trip," he said. "To Earth."

"Earth?"

"Yes. It seems as if there's a lot of interest in you at the moment, and the Navy has decided that as we served the public, it's their right to have access. We're going to be put on show." *Hell. Capgun was right.*

"And if the *Victory* gets called out while we're gone? I'm just a pilot, but you're the Stinger's CO."

"Then the XO will take the squadron," he said bitterly. "Not that a few people wouldn't welcome that."

Wrapped up in how that was going to affect her, she hadn't noticed that the CO didn't seem thrilled with the prospect, either. Right then, she knew that the rumored rift between the admiral and him was more than just a rumor.

"But, as I've been told, the risk of that is small. The *Victory* is getting some upgrades, which will take another few weeks, and Task Force Iron Sword is on the alert status. Along with half of the rest of the Navy, I might add.

"So, for the next two weeks, you and I will be performing dogs, showing off for the Navy, the latest bright new thing. You are, of course. Not me. I'm just there to give gravitas to the show."

He really is bitter.

"We're leaving at 2020, so go pack. Bring your pilot blues," he said, referring to the work overalls pilots wore aboard the ship, "your Class B's, and your Dress Blues."

"The chokers? This will be that formal?" she asked.

"Yes, that formal. You're going to meet the director."

"The director? As in the head of the Directorate?" she asked, mouth dropping open.

"The one and only."

Beth had briefly met the director a few times before for some holo-ops, but she still didn't know what to make of the man. For a petty officer to be around the most powerful human in the galaxy was heady stuff and something she'd just as soon skip.

"What does he want this time?" she asked, her eyebrows scrunching together.

He gave a little chuff of a laugh and said, "I guess I forgot to tell you about the main event. The director's going to be presenting you with your award." "Award, sir?" she asked.

She'd figured she'd be getting some sort of award, maybe another Platinum Star. But why would the director be the one pinning that on her? Besides, awards took their own sweet time making their way through the paperwork process.

"Yes, award. It's been rammed through the Directorate in record time, but you're to be awarded the big one."

"Sir? Which big one?"

"I should think that's obvious, Dalisay. You registered four kills in a single mission, and in the process, saved a planet.
You're getting the Order of Honor!"

Earth

Chapter 15

". . . great honor upon herself and the Navy of Humankind. Given under my hand, Kallas K. Strauss, Director of Humankind."

The director took the Order of Honor from the case a young, serious-looking aide was holding, and stepped up to Beth, placing the ribbon around her neck. The clasps connected with a soft click, the heavy medal settling just below her collarbones.

Which had been meticulously measured out prior to the ceremony. With Beth being so short, the regulation-length ribbon positioned the medal right at the swell of her breasts, and Captain Milsop almost had a conniption about that. Not good for the optics, he complained. Danielle, her personal handler, had to rush the OOH out to have the ribbon adjusted, getting it back just 20 minutes before the ceremony was to begin.

The director stepped back, then offered his hand.

"Congratulations, Petty Officer Dalisay," the director said as they shook, his trademarked crooked smile on his face. "But we've got to stop meeting like this. People will talk."

Beth dutifully gave a small laugh.

The director turned, still keeping her hand locked in his, so that the media could record them together. Beth had seen the director arrive backstage, a scowl on his face while he lectured a pale-faced woman, but now, in front of the crowd and the media. he beamed. It was as if someone had thrown a switch.

Beth tried to smile as the holocam operators went crazy, but the muscles in her face were shot. If that was even a thing.

Can someone pull a smiling muscle?

If they could, Beth was surely a candidate. For the last two weeks, she'd been marched out by the Navy brass like a prime pig, and the media had eaten it up. With the firm guidance from Captain Milsop and his team, they'd been fed a version of Beth's past that vaguely resembled reality, but impressed even her. She'd be in awe of this Floribeth Salinas O'Shea Dalisay, if that person existed.

The fact that this was Beth's second time in the media barrel made the interest even higher, if that was possible. The OOH was rare, but not unheard of. Five had been awarded since the first contact with the FALs. But couple her OOH and being the first Navy ace in 200 years, then add on that she'd been in the news less than a year ago, and Beth was approaching rock star status.

And she felt both undeserving and uncomfortable. She honestly hoped that her fifteen minutes would be over soon, and there would be someone else vaulted to the spotlight.

It wasn't that she didn't feel a sense of pride in what she'd done. Far from it. But the dog-and-pony-show aspect of it all was trying. She was a fighter pilot, and she wanted to be back with the squadron, doing her job. All of this was keeping her away.

Beth and the director stood there, hands still clasped, for a full minute, and their likenesses were recorded for posterity.

"You about done with this?" he whispered out of the corner of his mouth, his smile still cemented on.

"Yes, sir," Beth said, dropping her own smile for a moment before Captain Milsop gestured for her to plaster it back on.

"There's a lot of folks who want to congratulate you, young lady. You know, to get their holos taken with a real live hero. *Politicians*," he said with a tone of contempt, which Beth thought was rather interesting.

No, *hypocritical*. What was he doing if not the same thing?

"Let's you and I head back to the green room and chat for a bit. I can use the break."

And so could she. "Yes, sir, that would be great."

He finally dropped her hand and addressed the audience. "I know you're all anxious to congratulate Petty Officer Dalisay, but I'm invoking executive privilege here. I'm going to be stealing our hero here for a private meeting," he said, to the groans of some in the crowd.

"Don't worry. I'll have her back to you soon enough. Meanwhile, I'm sure Commander Tuominen will be happy to answer any questions you might have before you all head off to the reception. Just make sure you don't hog all of that delicious sisig we had brought in from New Cebu," he said, mispronouncing the dish, but raising a laugh. "Our hero said it was her favorite."

Beth had said no such thing. But it was her favorite dish from home, so someone had been doing their research. That felt decidedly creepy. What else did they know about her?

The commander and Captain Milsop stepped up together as the director and Beth, flanked by security, made their way offstage and down a non-descript hallway to the green room, the same one where Beth had waited prior to the ceremony. Security preceded them, scanning the room before allowing the director in.

The ever-present crooked smile faded, and his posture changed.

"I was told you liked Coke, right?" he asked before moving to the back table and pouring two glasses. He gave her one, then sat down across from her.

This was a different man. Not that he seemed upset, but he wasn't the smiling, grandfather-figure that he was on the stage. "So, you're flying back to the *Victory* tonight?"

"Yes, sir."

"I bet you're happy about that."

"Yes, sir. I'm anxious to get back. We've still got a job to do out there."

"You can take a break from all of that, Dalisay. Or can I call you Floribeth?"

"Most people call me Beth, sir."

"OK, Beth. I know you've been fed what to say on this junket, but you don't need that now with me, the 'still got a job' and all. Just relax."

Beth could feel her face redden. That was exactly one of the lines she'd been given. That didn't mean it wasn't true, though.

"Sorry, sir."

He waved her apology off.

"Just relax."

There was a knock, one of the secret servicemen opened the door, and one of the director's underlings came in, a silver bowl in his hand.

"Sir, I brought some of the sisig."

The director rolled his eyes and said, "Come on, Wilson. Really?"

"Sorry, sir. I didn't know if you were serious."

"You've been with me for two months now. You should know me better than that," the director said.

He started to wave his hand in dismissal when he stopped, looked at Beth, then asked, "Unless you want some?"

She knew what Captain Milsop would say about waiting for the director to eat first, but she hadn't eaten anything since a Breedlove Biscuit that morning, and she was hungry. Why should she demur just because she was with the big dog himself?

"Yes, sir. I would like some."

The director motioned to the table, where the aide dished out a plate and brought it to Beth before scurrying out the door. She dug in. It was surprisingly decent and hit the spot.

The director took one look at the sisig, then shrugged and leaned back in his chair, eyes closed. Beth wondered if he was asleep until she noticed his throat move in subvocalizations. The man was calling someone.

Beth finished her plate, then sat back, sipping her Coke, wondering what to do. The director was in deep conversation with someone, and she wasn't about to interrupt the man.

She held up her medal and examined it. She'd seen the one presented to Lieutenant Hadley's wife, but only from a distance. Up close, the life crystal that made up the medal's center was mesmerizing, the deep colors slowly shifting in never-ending patterns based on her own brainwaves. It was like an aurora captured in miniature. She could get lost in it.

With her crammed schedule, the fact that she was being awarded an OOH hadn't really sunk in. Holding it though, knowing that each medal was unique to the wearer, made it all real. She sucked in a breath, and the honor being bestowed upon her hit, and hit hard. She was almost overcome with the desire to get back in the *Tala* and earn that honor. It was almost painful to be sitting there, wasting time, while the director chatted with his lover, for all she knew.

Finally, after almost 20 minutes, the director opened his eyes and sat up.

"I think that's long enough to keep them waiting," he said.

"Are you about ready to meet the masses?"

He didn't really want to chat with me, she realized. *He just wanted the appearance of it.*

"Yes, sir," she said. She wasn't about to challenge the man on it. He was the director, after all, and he bled politics.

"OK, then," he said, standing up. Almost immediately, the door opened, and two secret servicemen flanked the door, looking at him expectantly.

"Then let's have at it." As he walked to the door, the other director, the one from all the holos Beth had seen of him, the one who pinned on her medal, seem to inflate and appear.

Beth normally kissed her cross when facing a tough task. This time, she lifted the OOH and kissed it before leaving the green room to face the gathered VIPs and media.

****

"It's been so good to work with you, Beth," Danielle said as she gave Beth a hug. "We're connected now, so keep in touch, OK?" "Sure will," Beth said.

And she planned to. Chief Danielle Han had been a welcomed surprise. A member of Captain Wilsop's PA team, she and Beth had hit it off, and the captain was smart enough to see that. He assigned Danielle as Beth's personal handler while he honchoed the overall two-week schedule.

As hectic as things were, the two had bonded, and Beth knew she was going to miss her. They held the hug a few more moments, then broke, but not before Danielle gave her a kiss on the cheek.

"Commander," she said, nodding to the CO before she walked out the door.

And that left Captain Milsop. The man had been tasked with making sure the tour went off without a hitch, and he'd mostly succeeded. Beth had recoiled at first when she found out that she and the CO were to be managed, but now, she was rather grateful that they had. It had made things much easier. All she had to do was show up, smile, and spout off one of her lines.

"You did well, Petty Officer Dalisay," he told her. "I'll make sure to mention that in my report. Have a safe trip back to the
Victory, OK?"

"I sure will, sir."

He shook her hand but didn't bother to acknowledge Commander Tuominen's presence before he left, leaving the two pilots in the VIP lounge, waiting for their shuttle.

"'I'll make sure to mention that in my report,'" the CO mimicked scornfully once the hatch closed. "As if anything he says matters."

There had been palpable tension between the two men the entire time together. The captain seemed like a competent, resourceful individual; however, he did seem to enjoy being in a position of authority over the CO; in particular, being in charge of a GT. Commander Tuominen was equally, if not more competent, but he was also a creature of privilege. He might have fought through the ranks to get to where he was now, but a lifetime of deference could not be erased. This had rarely, if ever, been a problem before, as far as Beth knew, but Captain Milsop's condescending attitude grated on her commander. The mere fact that he was babysitting Beth when he felt he should be back with the squadron just added fuel to the fire, and stoked his ill temper.

I just hope he doesn't blame me.

"We're done with him now, sir. It's back to the ship and the real Navy," she said, trying to support him.

"And we wonder what's wrong with the Navy," he muttered. "Damned staff pukes are going to be the death of us."

That might have been a little harsh. Beth had been happy that the "staff pukes" had taken care of all the arrangements. Danielle had been a godsend. She wasn't going to mention that though.

The CO looked at her, then smiled. "You're right, though. Back to the Stingers for us." He checked the time, then said, "We've got almost an hour. You up for a drink?"

"Uh . . . sure, sir," she said hesitantly.

Enlisted and officer might drink together at an official function, but not usually in a social setting, and with just the two of them, this sure felt like a social setting. The image of him kneeling between her legs to kiss her belly during the shellback ceremony flashed through her mind. That, and the command master chief's insinuation that there was something going on between the commander and her. She felt her face redden.

"What'll you have?" he asked, heading to the bar where a shiny robotender waited motionlessly.

"Just a beer, I guess, sir. A Tempest," trying to will her face back to normal.

He stopped and turned, shaking his head. "Come on, Dalisay. This is a fully-stocked bar. You can get your Tempest at any convenience store. How about something a little more daring?"

Beth didn't know what to say. On a E5's salary, beer and cider were the mainstays of her drinking. And if the CO disapproved of a Tempest, he certainly was not going to appreciate her ordering a screw-top Autumn Springs chardonnay. She thought for a moment, trying to recall from the holonovelas what the rich and famous drank.

"A Perseid Shower?" she finally asked.

The commander gave a slight nod, then turned to the robotender and said, "One Perseid Shower, with the Lednik Silver, for the lady. I'll have a Glenmorangie, neat."

"Right away, sir."

"This is all the real stuff, Dalisay. Nothing synthetic."

Beth nodded and kept silent, thinking that course of action better than talking and revealing her ignorance. She had no idea what a "Lednick Silver" was, nor a "Glenmor-whatever."

Within moments, the robotender delivered the two drinks.
Beth's was in a tall, fluted glass, just like on the holonovelas.
The commander's was in a short, cylindrical glass.

"To the Stingers," the commander said, raising a glass.

"To the Stingers," Beth echoed, clinking hers to his.

She looked inside the glass, gave it a sniff, then took a small sip. She had to hide back her disappointment. It tasted like a vodka and grapefruit juice to her, like her Auntie Clarabelle drank back in San Miguel.

This is supposed to be special?

It wasn't bad, but it didn't wow her. She took another sip, larger this time, then set the glass down on the bar.

"Your first Perseid Shower?" the commander asked.

She felt her face flush, but she looked him in the face and said yes.

"How do you like it?"

"It's . . . good."

"That's the Lednik. Best vodka in the spiral arm," he said.

"But a Perseid Shower's still a kid's drink. Candy in a glass."

"And what's that, sir?" she asked, pointing at his drink.

"Glenmorangie. Single Malt. From right here on Earth. Been around for centuries, and they know how to do it right. It's probably a little much for you, though."

Beth didn't like to be pigeon-holed, and she didn't like to be told what she could or couldn't do, what was good or bad for her.

Before she could stop it, her traitorous right hand reached out and snatched the drink from the startled commander's hand. She raised it to her lips, and looking him dead in the eye, took a long swallow . . .

. . . and almost choked. It was like drinking turpentine. She controlled her expression, though. She couldn't let him see he had been right. With an effort, she slowly smiled and handed the glass back to him.

What the hell, Floribeth? Just taking the CO's glass and drinking from it? What are you thinking?

"Not bad," she managed to get out, still watching his face for the explosion and dressing down she knew was coming.

Instead, he raised the glass in a toast to her, then downed the rest of the single malt.

"Impressive. The lady can handle her poison."

Almost spit it back out all over him, she thought, keeping a smile on her face.

"I'm in the Navy, sir," she said as if that was all the answer he needed.

"Touché, Dalisay, touché."

She looked over at the robotender, wondering if she should order something else. Not a Perseid Shower, and certainly not the Glenmorangie. But she didn't know when she'd be rubbing shoulders with societies elite again.

"I'd like something with a bit of a bite," she told the robotender. "Rum, maybe. Not too sweet."

"Do you like passion fruit?" the robotender asked.

She perked up. Passion fruit, or *massaflora* as they called it on New Cebu, was something of a luxury item. She'd had the artificial juice before, but the commander had said this bar didn't serve synthetics.

"Yes, I do," she said.

"Then may I suggest a Sunset Dream?"

She couldn't help but glance at the commander, who nodded.

Come on Floribeth, you don't need his approval, she scolded herself as she snapped back her line of sight.

"That would be fine."

The robotender pulled out a large tumbler before three tubular arms whipped out to dispense the liquids. A fourth arm dropped something in the top of the glass, then the bar top carried the drink to her. She picked it up and looked at it for a long moment.

Layered from reddish orange to a light yellow, gold flakes swirled in a tiny, slow tornado, kept moving by some unseen agitator. It was almost too pretty to drink.

Feeling the commander's eyes on her, she cut her gaze short and took a tentative sip . . . and almost immediately a much larger one. This was more like it. There was a hefty kick of highoctane rum, but it went down smoothly, balanced by the massaflora juice and something else she couldn't quite place.

"Good, right?" the commander asked. "Yes, sir. It's very good." *I could get used to this.*

"I'll take one, too," he told the robotender, then to Beth, "I haven't had a Sunset Dream in years."

He took a sip after the drink was delivered, nodded in appreciation, then asked Beth, "So, how were these last two weeks? Were you able to put up with the BS?"

Beth wasn't sure how to respond. The commander wasn't in a good mood, that was clear enough, but he didn't seem upset with her. Still, officers didn't tend to ask the enlisted what they thought of their duties. Orders were orders, and missions were missions. Beth would rather be with the squadron, but she'd had worse duties. The command master chief had seemed to relish assigning her to head-cleaning duties for her first six months with the squadron. And, to be honest, with Danielle running interference, it hadn't been that bad. Boring, yes.

Being put on display hadn't been fun.

But it had culminated in the Order of Honor, which went a long way in mitigating the "BS," as the commander called it. She glanced over to her carry-on bag, where she'd placed the medal itself after switching to the ribbon on her growing stack for the trip back to the *Victory*.

"Just following orders like a good little sailor, sir," she said.

"You and me both, Dalisay. You and me both."

He downed the drink in one big gulp, then ordered another. He had three times her mass, and he was evidently used to the effects. Beth was already feeling the buzz, so she slowed down. She was still on Earth, and she didn't need to be seen drunk, especially right after the ceremony.

The drinks did seem to loosen the commander up, even if he wasn't stumbling drunk. Emboldened by her own slight buzz, Beth asked him the question everyone in the squadron wanted to know, and he didn't seem to mind answering. The commander was part of the Tuominen clan, one of the most powerful in the Golden Tribe. What surprised Beth was that he was the son of Annukka Tuominen, putting him at the very pinnacle of power. He could be back on Karelia, enjoying a life of privilege that most norms could not even comprehend. Instead, he was driven by the need to prove himself as an individual, not as someone born into the position.

Beth listened as the commander, after switching back to single malts, told her about the resistance of his family to his serving in the Navy. That might be acceptable for some of the lesser cousins, but not one of the family primes.

One thing was certain, though. The commander was inordinately proud that he'd foreseen the need for the Stingers, and he'd used every contact and called in every favor to get them formed.

And luckily for humanity. While there had been indications that someone else was out there, not everyone had agreed with the necessity of something like the Stingers.

Beth had always respected him as her commander, but as she sipped her Sunset Dream, she realized she respected him as a person. Not as a GT, but as an individual.

She gazed at him as he told her about his mother, how she was pressuring him to come back home. Family problems, like any norm. Maybe GTs weren't really that different from norms.

He looked over at her and caught her gaze.

"What?" he asked, a small smile on his face.

What did the command master chief mean when she said I was his pet NEP? she wondered

"Sir, the shuttle will be here in ten minutes," a civilian said, poking her head in the door, and interrupting that dangerous line of thought.

"One more for the road, Dalisay?" he asked as the women closed the door.

She shrugged and said, "Sure." It would likely be her last opportunity to sample such high-end tipple. Mercy would renounce their friendship if she didn't take advantage of the situation.

They sat there in silence for a few moments, sipping their drinks, lost in their own thoughts, before the commander cleared his throat and asked, "What's it like, Dalisay?"

"Sir?"

"What does it feel like?"

"The OOH, sir? I'm honored, of course."

"No, not that," he said with a scowl. "I mean, splashing a FAL."

She was taken aback by the question, and it gave her pause.

What do I feel?

Beth could spout the "just doing my job" line, but she knew that wasn't what he was asking. She'd never thought about her kills in that frame of reference, though. How did she *feel*?

Beth considered it for a moment, thinking back, but she knew.

"Fucking great, sir. Better than about anything," she gushed, letting the feeling rush over her again in an almost physical wave. "Like I'm the most powerful person in the galaxy. I mean, it is my duty," she hurriedly said. "And I'm doing my job, but hell, I'd pay to do it, to be tested like that and come out on top, you know?"

She looked at him as he studied his empty glass, avoiding her gaze. And it hit her.

No, he didn't know. But she could see the longing in his body language. She could see the . . . not jealousy, but desire that bubbled within him, threatening to erupt.

Just like Mercy, he wanted to prove himself. Being a commander was not enough. Even as competent as he'd proven himself to be, he commanded the Stingers because of what he was, a GT, scion of one of the most powerful GT clans. But out there in the black, the crystals didn't care who he was. It was just him in his Wasp facing the enemy. And he wanted . . . no needed to prove himself in combat.

"It makes me whole, sir," Beth said quietly.

The commander nodded, saying nothing and refusing to meet her eyes, as if ashamed to have revealed a vulnerability. He turned his empty glass upside down on the bar.

This was good gossip, all of it, but Beth knew she'd never reveal what she'd learned about him. She knew what it was like to have a need to prove herself. She'd had that all her life, and it was the commander who'd given her the opportunity to do that. She owed him her discretion.

The shuttle arrived, and they boarded, sitting apart from each other. It was a quiet flight back to the *Victory*.

DS VICTORY

Chapter 16

"So, that's what they meant by the 'Pumpkin Ace?'" Beth asked Pork Chop. "That's pretty embarrassing.

Beth had been confused by some of crew referring to her as "Pumpkin" or "Pumpkin Ace." She'd finally asked Pork Chop about it, and he pulled up a holo of her at Mercy and Rocky's wedding. Not the one that had been retouched and distributed by the Navy, with her in her flight suit, but the real photo, the one with her in the orange bridesmaid dress.

"And everyone's seen that?" she asked.

"Pretty much the whole ship."

"Well, shit."

"Don't take it so hard. I mean, they're looking up to you," Pork Chop told her.

Beth wasn't so sure about that. The holo didn't shine her in the best light. She looked like a blooming idiot, not a warrior pilot.

Pork Chop seemed earnest about it, though. Then again, he was somewhat naive about the Navy. His life revolved around his Wasp, and not much beyond that.

Chief Petty Officer Enrique "Pork Chop" Bautista was a pilot for VF-51, the Exemplars. The squadron was newly attached to the *Victory* and Task Force Iron Shield. The Exemplars flew the Juliette version of the Wasp, not quite the FX6 Kilos that the Stingers flew, but the older frames, albeit with many of the same upgrades of the newer birds. Their addition gave the *Victory* 104 Wasps, a pretty potent hammer. Together with the monitors, the scouts, the Scarab assault craft, and the Marines, the ship could project power anywhere in the spiral arm. And that didn't include the other combatants and the huge *Chon Buri* support ship in the task force.

Beth had gravitated to Pork Chop the minute she met him. He was a fellow Pinoy, the first such pilot she'd met since leaving Hamdani Brothers. Not that they were from exactly the same background. Pork Chop was from the coastal city of General Santos, "GenSan," back in the Philippines on Earth. Beth was from New Cebu, one of several diaspora worlds. Time and distance resulted in "parsec drift," changes in a culture that could be a bit disconcerting at times. But the core of their backgrounds was the same, and that was enough, and they'd become friends.

It didn't hurt that even if Pork Chop was a chief, two grades above her, he was somewhat deferential to her. That's what being an ace gave a pilot, she figured. But Pork Chop also told her that she was a big deal within the Filipino community. That both surprised and pleased her. It also made her more than a bit nervous, having to live up to an entire people's expectations.

And Floribeth Dalisay, Navy Ace, sounded better than the "Pumpkin Ace." Much more gravitas.

But Pork Chop assured her that the real holo had only been seen on the ship. Beth hoped it was true, but in her experience, no secret could ever be kept from the prying eyes of the public.

Chapter 17

"So, are those our replacements?" Capgun asked as the pilots watched the first of the new Dragonfly Drones being guided to the rails by the yellowshirt team.

"They can never replace human pilots," Mercy said with conviction.

"Never say never," Beth said. "Besides, they have pilots," she added, nodding at the group of drone operators who were watching the proceedings intently.

"Them? Yeah, right," Mercy said. "As if."

Except, technically, they were pilots. At the least the Navy considered them so. The drones might be far more automated than a Wasp, but the pilots/operators still gave the inputs to the drones' AIs, the human element in the operations chain.

The four of them were not the only Stingers observing the test launch. It looked like the entire squadron just happened to be wandering around Bravo Hangar when the drone fighters were to be given their launch check.

"They don't look like much," Josh said, the disdain evident in his voice. If anything, her plane captain was more against the unmanned drone's presence than the pilots.

And he was right. Each drone was a sphere, a little over two meters in diameter. Mostly featureless and without visible engine ports, there was little to indicate that the drones were fully functional spaceships. But it did have an engine, a compact FC engine that had the same output as a Wasp's. Unlike a Wasp, though, the thrust was not simply vectored, which had mechanical limitations. It could be routed through any one of 64 ports spread out across the drone's skin, each hidden by a door until activated.

The advantage? Thrust could be directed immediately in any direction, and without a human body to protect, the drone could handle extreme G-forces. In other words, they were far, far more maneuverable than Wasps.

The drones were the latest generation, the finest ever produced. The Navy had traditionally resisted using drones as fighter pilots—many people holding that was because pilots were too politically powerful within the Navy. They didn't want to lose their *raison d'etre*.

Beth didn't know if there was any truth to things so high above her pay grade. But the fact that the squadron had been assigned to the *Victory* was proof enough that the powers that be thought they needed every advantage to combat the crystal threat.

The *Victory* was now bursting at the seams with the Exemplars and now the drone squadron joining the rest of the ship's complement. The Victory's own weapons systems had all been upgraded as well. Along with the other ships, the task force was loaded for bear.

There was an undercurrent of anticipation that was flowing through the crew. This wasn't for show. The directorate didn't gather so many resources in one place unless they were going to be used.

The question on everyone's mind was just how that was going to happen.

Chapter 18

Three weeks later, the question had only been partially answered. The *Victory* and the reconstituted Task Force Iron Shield were underway again. Not only TF Iron Shield, but three others as well, all slowly—cautiously—pushing forward into the inner arm.

There might be four task forces taking part in Operation Eagle Sweep, but at the squadron level, there wasn't any indication of coordination with the other three. Maybe Commander Tuominen was being briefed on the big picture, but for the rest of the pilots and crew, this was no different than their previous deployment. The task force was jumping from one location to the other, based on the main Navy threat AIs' calculations on where the FALs were hiding.

"Hiding" was the operative word. There hadn't been a crystal sighting, much less an attack, for close to a month.

"Think we'll hit paydirt this time?" Mercy asked Beth on the S2S.

"Probably not. Why should this be any different? What's it been? Nine jumps? And all we do is sit here watching a gate until the scout returns."

There had been some changes in the SOP as a result of losing a scout on the last deployment. First, there were now four scouts with the task force. And no longer did they go off in their Mosquitoes alone to recon the Area of Interest. They were always escorted by a flight of Wasps.

Not that the Wasps would actually enter the AOI. A Mosquito was a super-stealthy ship. A Wasp, while it didn't have a huge signature, was not. Reconning space demanded invisibility, or as close to it as humanity could create. So, Mosquito and Wasps jumped together to what was essentially a staging area, then the scout jumped again to the AOI while the Wasps took up a circular station, making sure that at least one Wasp was always in position to jump if necessary.

Sitting and waiting was wearing on the pilots. To a person, they wanted to engage. And so far, they hadn't found a trace of a FAL, despite the AIs' giving high probability of crystal presence.

"I hope Aztec finds something. My trigger finger is getting itchy. I need to splash something," Mercy said.

One evolution with the Wasps accompanying the Mosquitos was that the pilots were far more integrated with the rest of the crew. "Aztec" was Lieutenant Commander Nick Delagrosso, the scout detachment's second-in-command.

"It's going to be another dry hole. Mark my words," Beth grumbled.

"How are you holding up, Dalisay?" the commander asked over the S2S.

Beth almost jumped.

Has he been listening in to my bitching? she wondered guiltily.

An S2S was supposedly private, but the commander, who'd decided to accompany Fox Flight, had more comms authority and probably could listen in to any conversations, even on the private comms link.

"I'm fine sir," she said in what she hoped was a neutral tone. "Ready for whatever comes our way."

"I know this is getting old, but at some point, we're going to find them."

He sounded more wistful than hopeful. It was common knowledge that he and the commodore did not get along well, and Beth felt a tug of empathy for the man. It was no wonder why he wanted to get off the ship and out into the clean vacuum of space. He was an outsider, just as Beth was. He might be privileged in society while Beth was from the lower social economic strata, but they were still different from the rest. And while Beth had been able to integrate herself with the other pilots, the commander, being the commander, had not. They said command was lonely, and Beth believed it.

She wanted to say something, to let him know she understood. But Beth had been careful around the commander since their return, especially considering the command master chief's accusation. The commander had been more attentive to her, even to the extent of calling her Beth on occasion. He hadn't crossed any line, but his attitude toward her had shifted just enough for Beth to wonder if the command master chief was right.

Beth could hear the weariness in his voice, however. She had to say something.

"How are you holding up, sir?"

Oh, that really helped, Floribeth. Is that the best you could come up with?

"I'm OK, thanks. I'd be better without this damned neckcracker," he said with a laugh.

"Sir?"

"Oh, nothing, nothing. Just joking."

It took Beth a moment to process that. The commander was tall, twice as tall as Beth, and he'd had to pull GT strings to get a waiver to fly Wasps. He'd always had to be a contortionist just to get into the cockpit, and that was before the neck-crackers had been issued. The big helmets were bulky even for the other pilots. Capgun kept complaining that his kept hitting the inside of the *Lovely Rita's* canopy. With the commander, it had to be worse.

He must be all sorts of squished in there.

"Well, Aztec will be back soon, and we'll get back to the *Victory*."

"Yeah. Goody," he blurted out, then, "I mean, yes. We'll be back and getting our next mission. You hang in there, Dalisay.
We'll find the FALs."

He cut off the connection.

"Mercy, did the commander ask you how you were doing?" Beth asked after a few moments. "No, why?"

"Oh, nothing. Just wondering."

"He's just along for the ride. Probably needed to get off the ship and out of the commodore's sight for awhile. Don't blame him much, even for this boring shit."

"Yeah, I guess so," Beth said. "Well, I'm up again. Let me check my readings."

The *Tala* was looping around again, entering her window of being in position to shoot the gate. This looping formation was the easiest way to allow the Wasps to keep up their speed but be in position to jump. Beth didn't really need to check her readings. The *Tala's* AI would let her know if something was wrong, but years in the decidedly lower-tech Hummingbirds as a commercial exploratory scout had ingrained the habit into her.

She'd just confirmed the readings when Aztec's broke into the flight net and passed, "Stinger One, I've got multiple bogies on my tail. Coming in hot."

Beth's heart jumped as the data appeared on the inside of her neck-cracker.

"Roger that," both Gollum and the commander passed simultaneously. With the commander just there as an observer, Gollum was "Stinger One," not the commander.

Aztec was running for his life with what looked to be at least a dozen FALs flickering in and out of the display. Beth held her breath, waiting for the order to shoot the gate while her AI started processing targeting data.

"Fire Ant, go. The rest of us, adjust and get through the gate as fast as possible, then synch. I want to cover Aztec and get him back. That's the priority, not engaging the FALs." "I'm coming, too," the commander passed.

Beth inputted the order while she waited to hear what Gollum said to that. The commander had not worked together with Fox Flight, and Gollum was hell on coordinated actions. Technically, as the mission commander, he could tell the skipper to hold back. But Commander Tuominen was his boss, and it would be hard to tell him no.

"Roger that, Obsidian. Take the Echo position."

Beth accelerated as she approached the gate. She mimed kissing her cross as she jumped into a new system, a gas giant visible as a bright star in the distance, leaving the others behind. She put the *Tala* into a K-drift that would start spinning her around to reenter the gate, but with her between Aztec and the pursuing FALs.

She fired her L-40 lasers at the lead of what she now saw were 13 FALs. The lasers had not proven to be effective against crystal ships, but Beth wanted them to see her and hopefully take away attention from Aztec, but while not wasting her torps or hadron cannon at the extreme range.

"Sure glad to see you, Stinger-Four," Aztec said.

"Happy to oblige, Aztec."

Behind her, Gollum shot the gate. He immediately started moving into the Slot B position. At this point, this was not seatof-the-pants-flying. With two Wasps in system now, the AIs were working overtime, calculating the optimal positioning, given the mission and enemy disposition. Beth had initiated the K-drift, but now she had to suppress the urge to take over from the AIs.

Of course, her urge was to close in with the enemy and take them on. But that wasn't the mission.

Gollum, the commander, and then Mercy followed, each Wasp moving into position.

Ahead of them, the FALs didn't break their course. They seemed intent on chasing down Aztec and his Mosquito. A Mosquito was fast, but four of the crystal ships seemed to be closing the distance, leaving the rest behind.

Some sort of super-FAL?

"Mozzie-One, just keep it steady for the gate. We'll keep the FALs off your ass," Gollum told Aztec.

"Roger that. Sorry about the short notice. They just sort of appeared on me."

"No problem. You just get to the gate."

Then it was nail-biting time. It was thirty-one minutes before the *Tala* slid into position between the scout and the FALs. The four lead crystal ships were just within range of the torps. Beth knew the mission was to get the scout back, but still

. . .

"I want to take a shot at the lead three FALs. Give them something to think about," she passed on the flight net.

It took a moment, but Gollum finally said, "Go ahead. One torp."

All of the Wasps had the 57-Ns, the production designations of the 57-Xs she'd tested at SG-62998. Beth targeted the lead FAL and fired.

Within moments, the four FALs started to spread apart. Lances of their energy beams reached out, converging onto the torpedo. One beam hit the *Tala* for a few moments, but her shields held.

"Damn, sista. You sure got their attention," Mercy told her. "But save some for me."

"There's plenty for both of us."

Gollum was already sliding into position. He started putting out blasts from his P-13, adding to the barrage. The more they could get the FALs to react, the less attention they'd be giving to Aztec.

The FAL assault on her torpedo paid off for the crystals. It went skipping off course, a clean miss.

Beth kept running the numbers. Unless the FALs had something new up their sleeves, Aztec should be able to reach the gate before the enemy would be within effective range.

As if to punish her for thinking that thought, the gods of war decided to act. Three FALs winked into existence . . . on the *other* side of the gate and racing back toward them.

Alarms went off as Gollum ordered Beth and Capgun forward to try to intercept the three. Which was problematic. Aztec was between the three and the new FALs. There was no way they could get between them. They had to rely on their weaponry, firing past the Mosquito.

"Aztec, shift to course zero-six-four-two, niner-three-threethree, seven-one-zero-one for one-twenty seconds," Gollum ordered. "Then adjust back to the gate and make a run for it."

"Roger that," Aztec passed. A moment later, the Mosquito started to drift slightly off its previous course.

"Commence fire with your beamers and L-40s," he ordered Capgun and Beth.

"L-40s?" asked Capgun.

"Affirmative. Catch their attention."

The laser beam traveled at the speed of light, faster than any of the other weapons, but the weapon hadn't been effective against the crystal ships. Beth had fired hers as soon as she shot the gate to get the FALs' attention, but now, she thought firing them was a waste of power, adding to the heat build up. Orders were orders, though. She left the L-40 on auto, then turned to her hadron cannon, attempting to focus the beams for maximum effect at the oncoming FALs' range.

The FALs took notice. The Wasps' quantum scanners detected power blossoms. Even at this close range, it would still take the beams themselves ten to twelve seconds to reach them, enough time to take evasive action. All three jinked, and the crystal beams missed.

The FALs were not passively approaching, waiting to be hit, either. They dodged out of the way as well. As the range closed, the delay between firing and the weapons hitting was going to get less and less.

But firing seemed to be having the desired outcome. As Aztec drifted to the side, the FALs now seemed focused on the three Wasps charging them.

Mercy and the commander were bringing up the rear, oriented to the pursuing FALs. Mercy had now fired two torps, the commander one. None of the three hit its target, but they made the FALs react, widening the gap between them. It if was just those 13, then the humans would be home free. But it wasn't just them.

"Let's see if we can trap them," Gollum told them, sending over three torpedo attack routes. "On my command . . ." he started, giving Beth and Capgun time to download their route into a M-57, "Fire!"

The torpedoes took off, each in a slightly different direction, all at the designated crystal ship. The torps, accelerating at a rate that no human could survive, even under G-Shot, would still take over a minute to reach the FALs.

With 120 seconds gone, Aztec changed course again, now heading back to the gate again. The oncoming FALs didn't seem to react to him.

"Think they know where the gate is?" Beth asked Capgun as she initiated ejecting her first string of fire turds, wanting to keep on top of heat dissipation.

"I doubt it. We can't see the gate from the far side unless we're right on top of it."

"Just seems like an awful coincidence that they popped up on the other side."

"Coincidence, or they wanted to block off our direction of flight?"

"Maybe," Beth said, not convinced.

"Bet you a beer my torp hits," Capgun said as the M-57s sped to their target.

"You're on," Beth said, keeping up the beamer fire.

By coming in from different angles, the hope was that the FAL couldn't dodge all three.

It couldn't. Beth's torp was taken out, just a kinetic missile with no maneuverability. Gollum's torp detonated, but too far away to do damage as the target jinked, but that took it right into Capgun's torp. The crystal ship exploded into a cloud of particles.

"Yeah, baby!" Capgun shouted in unbridled excitement. "I'm a fucking ace!"

"Good shooting, but hold off on the celebrations. We're not out of this yet," Gollum told him.

"Congrats," Beth passed quickly on the S2S. But the flight commander was right. There were still two FALs heading right at them.

With the range closing, things began to happen at a quicker pace. The *Tala* was under fire, her shields degrading, but she was dishing out beamer fire on the FAL on her right. It was a battle of endurance now, of whose shield would last the longest.

Beth was just about to fire her last torpedo when Capgun fired his. The beam on her shifted to target the torp, and Beth continued to pour fire onto the opponent. Her temps were redlining, but she held firm, not wanting to shunt any power from her cannon with more fireturds.

She began to fear that she'd pass the oncoming FAL, and she started to tell Mercy to be ready to engage it when it went dead. No explosion, just dead. She'd probably just registered her eighth kill. "Probably" because it could be playing possum. If it were a human ship, that would be a real possibility. The FALs had never played possum before, but they'd been showing quite a bit of new tactics.

"Keep and eye on Alpha-fifteen," she told Mercy. "I think it's dead, but you never know."

Mercy clicked on an acknowledgment, but didn't say anything. She was probably upset that Beth had gotten yet another kill while she was still at zero. Beth didn't have time to worry about that, however. This was war.

The commander splashed the last of the three FALs, and the way to the gate was clear.

"Fire Ant, loop with me to flank the commander. Capgun, take Aztec through the gate," Gollum ordered.

"But—" Capgun started before being cut off.

"You're Winchester, Capgun. Take it back."

Which wasn't entirely true. Capgun had his hadron cannon, he had his railgun. But he was out of his M-57s, while Beth still had one left.

"Roger that."

Beth was already in a tight loop, her cannon already firing at the pursuing FALs. Her shields were already down to 62%, but the commander was down to 47%. He'd emptied his tubes at the pursuit without effect, and he and Mercy were taking the combined fire from 13 crystal ships.

None of the lead four FALs reacted to her, instead, they kept targeting the commander and Mercy. Both were evading the beams the best they could while giving back as good as they received, but with four against two, they were on the weak end of the stick.

Not four against two. Four against four now.

Just over two minutes after she and Gollum started back, first Aztec, then Capgun, shot the gate. Aztec would continue through the next gate and back to the *Victory*, while Capgun would wait, ready to destroy this gate as soon as the four Wasps shot it.

They just had to get to the gate in one piece. Beth ran the numbers, and they should be fine, shooting the gate with time to spare.

Beth and Gollum slid into position, flanking the other two Wasps. They both started to draw some fire, but their shields were holding. Just a straight shot to the gate and then through. Beth's stomach gave a lurch when two torpedoes were fired at them, but by shifting their cannon fires, they were able to knock them out before they got too close.

"Obsidian, watch your temps," Gollum passed.

Beth pulled up the commander's readout. His Wasp was well past the redline, and that was affecting its performance. His acceleration was slipping.

"I've got it," the commander passed. "That slipped past me."

A moment later, fireturds started pouring out of his fighter, and slowly, his temps started to fall. Beth wasn't sure how he'd missed that. His helmet display should have been blaring away. "Sir, did you take off your neck-cracker?" she passed on the S2S.

There was a pause, then he came back with, "I had to. I couldn't function anymore."

Crap! But how is he . . .

The comms went through both a cockpit speaker and the helmet. But if his neck-cracker was still hardwired in, then the canopy display would be off, and he wouldn't have heard any alarms. So, if the displays . . .

"Is your helmet still hardwired? Are you flying on autopilot?"

There was a longer pause, then, "I had to, Beth. Too many hours crammed in here. My body was cramping."

Commander Tuominen had essentially taken himself out of the equation. His Wasp might as well be a drone, the very thing that the body of Navy pilots was fighting against.

Neither the autopilot or weapons AI were connected to the fireturds, though, which had been an add-on, so, with the commander out of the loop, his Wasp's temps had gotten too high.

"Get that helmet back on! Or at least disconnect the hardwire!" Beth shouted at him, disregarding their difference in rank.

"I've got it disconnected. I don't know why I didn't before."

He didn't because his body is rebelling against being folded up like origami. This is bad.

At least now, he'd have a better picture of the situation, and he could jump in when needed. He shouldn't have been on the mission, and once his body started to act up, he should have pulled out. Beth was going to give him an ass-chewing when they got back, commander or not.

"We've got a problem here," she passed to Gollum on the S2S. "The commander's on autopilot. He's got . . . he's got physical problems."

"What? Why didn't he say something? I don't see anything here on his biodata."

"It's real."

And as wolves attack the weakest caribou, the FALs, seeing the commander's drop in acceleration, took that moment to pounce. Four torpedoes were fired, each spread out, but Beth didn't need to see the AI's analysis to know the commander was the target. Just as when Capgun splashed the crystal ship, the FALs were sending their torps to come in from different directions to increase the odds for a hit.

"You've got incoming," she told the commander.

"I see them."

Gollum immediately assigned each Wasp one of the incoming crystal torps. Beth's universe narrowed down to her target, ignoring the beamers that still slammed against her shields, ignoring the FALs that were firing them. Everything was that single torpedo hurtling towards the commander. Despite being locked onto it, the round torp kept coming. She kept waiting for it to detonate, to go dead, but it kept advancing. At twenty seconds out, Beth fired her last torpedo and readied her railgun, hoping for a similar miracle shot like the one at New Cebu.

Her M-57 ran true, however, impacting the FAL torpedo seven seconds out. She shifted her focus to the others, ready to fire her rail gun, just in time to see the last incoming torpedo explode close—too close—to the commander. But his icon was still there, and she let out a sigh of relief.

Too soon.

"I've taken damage. My FC is out," the commander passed on the flight net, his voice unnaturally calm.

FUCK!

She looked closer at his readouts. His cockpit was intact, and he was not hurt. But his FC engine had kicked out. And without his engine, he had no power to accelerate, no power to fire his weaponry. He just had ten hours or so for life support.

Without power, he'd just keep on a straight line forever.

"Fire Ant, Red Devil, take him in a dual tractor and shoot the gate," Gollum passed. "I've got your six."

"What? We've got no time," Mercy protested.

"So, you'd better not waste any of it, right. Do it now."

Beth reacted immediately, taking control and swinging the *Tala* into the commander's Wasp.

A dual tractor was occasionally used in orbit for smaller ships to horse larger ones around in-system. It wasn't used by fighters, and it wasn't used at high speeds. Mercy was right about the time, too. At their present speed, they'd hit the gate in less than six minutes, way too short of a time to grab his Wasp. But they had to try. The mini-gate Aztec emplaced had to be hit precisely. It took minute adjustments all the way to the gate, and the commander's Wasp couldn't maneuver. His present course was only approximate, with a one-in-a-million chance that it was exactly on target.

Beth was tempted to G-Shot to reach the commander, but she needed her full wits if they were going to pull this off. She pushed the *Tala* to the limits of human endurance, closing the gap while staring at her helmet display to pick him up on visuals. She kept up a series of grunts, tensing her belly, to keep conscious.

The *Tala* shot ahead, closing the distance, but she still had to decelerate to match his speed. At the halfway point, she flipped and started the process, all the time watching the timer tick down. It was going too quickly. They wouldn't make it.

"Gollum's turning," Mercy passed.

Beth took her attention off the commander for a moment. Mercy was right. The flight leader was turning to face the still oncoming FALs and decelerating, which had the effect of closing the distance.

"Gollum!" Beth shouted over the flight net. "What are you doing?"

"You just get the commander out of here," he answered.

She wanted to argue, but she couldn't afford the time, not if she was going to get Commander Tuominen through the gate.

Within seconds, his Wasp was visible as she started to bring the *Tala* to the favored belly-to-belly position.

"I'm getting ready to activate the grappling hook," she passed to the commander.

"I'm pleased to see you," he said calmly, making Beth laugh out loud at his understatement.

Which was good for her, clearing some of her panic.

"I'm here, too," Mercy said. "Where?"

The grappling hook worked best from a belly to belly aspect, but it could grasp at any point on a Wasp's skin. Beth thought for a moment. The rapidly approaching gate was small, so a smaller profile would be better.

"Right on top of him, Mercy," she said. "But make it quick.
We've got . . . fifty-three seconds."

Setting the grappling hooks normally was a meticulous, planned evolution that could take several minutes. That was a non-starter here. If they missed the gate, there was no way in hell that they could come back again, tractoring the commander, with 13 FALs on their tails. This was a one-shot attempt.

"Connecting now," Beth said as soon as she eased into range.

Her grappling hook shot out, the beam settling on the belly pad. She held her breath until the LED flashed green. She had a connection. Slowly, afraid to break the beam, she pulled the commander in close, until with a shudder, they made physical contact. She didn't need that—in fact, actually touching was usually avoided, but she was afraid of the small gate size.

Immediately, she checked their approach and started making the minute corrections necessary to hit the gate correctly . . . and almost broke the connection. The tractor beam worked with gentle adjustments at these speeds. "Help me, Mercy! Get connected." "Connecting now," her friend said.

A moment later, her grappling beam caught. It wasn't as good a connection as Beth had, but it was steady.

"Pull in close," Beth told her. "Until you're touching. You won't damage it." *I hope.*

"Then slave off of my AI. We'll need both of us.

She looked back at the timer.

Twenty-two seconds.

They were still off course. Close, but that wouldn't make a difference.

"Get him through," Gollum passed.

Beth didn't have time to answer. She nudged the threesome slightly, hoping to bring them into the cone. It wasn't enough.

Thirteen seconds.

"Beth!" Mercy shouted over the net. "Get us there!"

The commander stayed silent as Beth fed in another course correction. If it was just the *Tala*, it would be easy. But she had to fight the grappling hooks and the mass of two more fighters.

Still not enough! Come on Floribeth!

Five . . . four . . .

"Shit, shit, shit! We're not—" Mercy started yelling.

Beth didn't have time to run another calculation. She just acted, manually goosing the *Tala*—and the other two—over just a bit as she reached through the neck seal of her neck-cracker and grabbed for the silver cross hanging around her neck, jerking it out from under her flight suit. *two . . . one . . .*

. . . and they shot through the gate.

Beth stared at her display, not daring to believe they'd made it, that they were parsecs away in another section of space. She raised the cross to her lips and kissed it, giving Ave Maria a prayer of thanks.

"My fucking god," Mercy said, her voice high with relief. "Could you cut it any closer, sista?"

"You OK, sir?" Capgun asked, cutting in.

"I'm fine, thanks to Dalisay and Hamlin. Physically fine. The *Kalma* is DIS."

"I'm glad to hear you're OK, sir. Mercy, Beth, get the commander to the next gate. I'm blowing this one." "No!" Mercy and Beth shouted in unison.

"Gollum's still there," Beth said. "We need to wait for him."

"No, he's not," Capgun said somberly. "He didn't make it."

"But he just spoke to us not twenty seconds ago," Beth protested, pulling up her display.

The *Tala* still had eyes on the other side through the gate. There were the FALs, still rushing forward, but no Gollum. He was gone.

Beth felt a dagger tear at her heart, and tears welled in her eyes. He could have made it out. They all could have, if it weren't for the commander and his ego, placing them all in danger. She wanted to lash out, and she blamed him.

"Beth, take the commander back. Gollum knew what he was doing. He told me to blow the gate as soon as you made it."

Beth's heart was both broken and full of angry fire at the same time. It took an effort of will to calm down. Capgun was right. First and foremost, he had to destroy the gate.

She took several deep breaths, trying to force her mind back to the mission. She entered the coordinates of the next gate, and hit "execute."

They still had a long trip back to the *Victory*.

Chapter 19

"It's official," Wingnut said, sticking his head into Mercy and Beth's stateroom. "He's off flight status. Grounded."

"What about command?" Mercy asked. "Is he still in charge?"

"As of now, yes. But who knows? There's going to be an inquiry. They'll make a decision on what to do after that."

"Thanks," Beth said as the chief warrant officer went to spread the word.

Beth didn't know what she felt about it. About the commander. She'd been angry with him after they jumped. If he hadn't been there, Gollum would still be alive. But as they slowly made their way in silence to the next gate, she had time to think. "If this" and "if that" could be debated forever. They'd lost other pilots before, and they'd lose more before the FALs could be defeated and sent back to whatever cesspool of a planet begat their sorry existence.

The commander might not be the best pilot, and he probably shouldn't be flying, but the Stingers owed their very existence to him. He alone had the foresight to create the squadron, giving humanity a huge leg up in fighting the crystals.

"You know they're going to cover it up," Mercy said. "The fucking GTs won't let one of their own look bad."

Beth wasn't so sure about that. She knew about his relationship with his mother. She'd probably welcome his failure, knowing that with no more future in the Navy, it would force him back to the family fold. She couldn't disclose that to Mercy, however, without revealing how she knew that. And she wasn't ready to share what the commander had told her in what she assumed to be in confidence.

No, Commander Tuominen, "Obsidian," should not fly. But he shouldn't be cashiered in disgrace, either. The Navy needed him to exert influence to make sure it received the support it needed as it continued to gear up for the war.

Chapter 20

Even with the skipper off flight status, not much changed in the squadron. The scouts, accompanied by a flight of Wasps, tried to track down contacts, usually hitting dry wells. Twice, there was contact, with the scouts making it back in one piece. But for the most part, it seemed to be an exercise in futility. The task force, with eleven capital ships and two support ships, was a prize-fighter looking for a fight, but with no one stepping into the ring.

The XO became the nominal Fox Flight team leader, but with the skipper off flight status, the XO took over his flying duties as well, leaving Capgun in charge of the three-plane flight.

Frustration, tinged with a heavy dose of boredom, crept over the crew. Fights breaking out were a common occurrence. The finely-honed sword was getting dulled. The only cure would be combat, but the FALs weren't cooperating.

They were getting more active, though, hitting civilian ships, attacking planets, but running before the Navy could mount a counterattack. With four task forces in Operation Eagle Sweep, not one had become decisively engaged. But each contact—or supposed contact—sucked the task forces farther and farther inside the spiral arm, and farther and farther from each other. With gate technology, that wasn't a huge strategic vulnerability, but it was mentally trying, knowing that even as powerful as each task force was, they were all minuscule specks in the galactic scheme of things.

Something had to break, and break soon.

✳✳✳✳✳✳✳✳✳✳✳✳✳✳✳✳

"General quarters, general quarters. All hands, man your battle stations."

Beth, Mercy, Josh, and Pork Chop were in the two friend's stateroom, playing Pick Eight, when the call to general quarters filled the ship. Within moments, the four were moving to their assigned station: Mercy and Beth to the Stinger's ready room, Josh to the *Tala*, and Pork Chop to the Exemplar's ready room.

"Another drill?" Mercy asked as they ran through the corridor.

"Could be," Beth said, but something in her gut told her this was the real thing. Finally, they were going into action.

If there was any doubt, as they ran into the ready room, the mass of bodies getting dressed dispelled that notion. This was the real deal.

"Listen up!" Jumpman, the Bravo Flight commander and the squadron operations officer yelled out. "The skipper will be here in ten mikes. Everyone get dressed and grab a seat. We're going FAL-hunting!"

A cheer filled the room.

Beth slipped out of her overalls, then pulled the inner harness over her long johns. She hit the connectors that fitted the plumbing to the right orifice as well as the body monitors, then pulled her flight suit off the rack. Three minutes after arriving, she was ready.

She gave Mercy a loud slap on the ass, saying, "Too slow, sista," as she moved past her friend and to her seat.

Theories were running wild as pilots guessed as to what was going on. The "general quarters" indicated that it was something big, though.

****

It was closer to 15 minutes before the skipper and the command master chief arrived. It was odd to see the commander in his pilot blues, the ubiquitous overalls they all wore on the ship instead of a flight suit.

The room immediately quieted down, and the skipper spoke up, eschewing the mic.

"A large contingent of crystals has attacked a research station on Tantulus Five."

Beth had no idea where Tanatalus Five was, and she wasn't going to look it up now.

"They have also launched another attack on the mining operation in the Moapa system.

That was the second system drawing a blank with her. She didn't care, though, where they were, just that they could trap the FALs there.

"The directorate has ordered the Navy to crush both attacking forces, and Task Force Iron Shield has been given the mission to destroy the crystal force at Tantulus Five."

There was another cheer, and the commander held up his hand to quiet everyone.

"The counterattack is being led by the *Stephens*, the *Silver Mountain*, and two monitors," he said to the intake of breath from the pilots.

The *Stephens* was a heavy destroyer, the *Silver Mountain* a frigate. This was the first time capital ships had been ordered into direct battle. They all knew it was bound to happen, but a turning point had been reached. The Wasps may still be the tip of the spear, but they were no longer the entire weapon.

Perhaps more pertinent, it was obvious that the directorate was beyond the probing phase, dogfights scattered around the galaxy. They wanted to move the conflict into total war, holding nothing back.

Beth almost missed the next thing the commander said.

"The Exemplars will be escorting the capital ships into battle."

There was a chorus of protests, and the command master chief had to shout "At ease, at ease."

"I know you expected something different, but they have to be blooded. This will be a two-stage jump, and the Stingers will be the security element in the transit point, ready to jump into the Tantulus system the moment it is needed.

"The XO will be leading our mission. We're running very short of time, so there won't be a formal operations order. It's being uploaded to your Wasps now.

"I won't be out there with you this time, but I'll be in the CIC here on the *Victory*, monitoring your progress. You have my utmost confidence.

"Stingers!"

"Stingers!" the gathered pilots shouted back as they stood. Within moments, it was asses and elbows as they rushed out of the ready room and to their birds.

Chapter 21

"Well, this sucks hind tit," Mercy groused for the twentieth time.

Beth agreed with her sister-in-law. That was a succinct description of their situation. Not only were they not in the transit point, Fox Flight, with its three Wasps, and Hotel, with four, never made the first jump. They were held back with the bulk of the task force as a security patrol.

"How the hell am I going to get a kill if they won't let me fight?"

Beth had more kills than any other living pilot, but she still felt a strong degree of empathy with Mercy. She kept waiting, hoping for the call to go forward. This was the start of the real, total war, and they were sitting it out.

Even the Marines had gone forward, and least a company of the grunts. The rest were cooling their heels in the *Victory*, waiting for the war to come to them. Not that it would be any time soon. The flagship, surrounded by nine capital ships, three support vessels, four flights of drones—and seven Wasps—were two jumps back from the battle in a secure sector. The admiral was directing the battle from the ship's CIC with her staff, but the rest of those in the rear could only follow what was happening in bits and pieces when someone bothered to report it to them.

"Your time will come, Mercy," Beth said.

"Easy for you to say," Mercy snapped, followed by pause, then a, "Sorry, Beth. I didn't mean that."

"Don't worry about it. I know you didn't mean anything by it," Beth told her.

I just hope she gets a kill soon and gets the jealousy out of her system.

So far, though, in each of her fights, it had been Mercy who almost bought the farm, and that thought scared Beth.

Not just for her, but for Rocky. She couldn't imagine how he'd cope with losing Mercy.

"Fox and Hotel, here's an update," Commander Tuominen broke into the net. "The forward element successfully caught the FALs while they were still in system. The FALs are now in flight mode with our forces in pursuit. It's much the same with Task Force Iron Lance in the Moapa system. This a good day for the Navy. A great day.

"I'll keep you updated as I can," he said before leaving the net.

"That's . . . that's great news. But I sure the hell wish we were there," Mixmaster, the Hotel Flight team leader passed.

"You've got that right," Mercy chimed in.

Beth felt the same, but she keyed her mic and passed, "Whether we're in on this fight or not, maybe this is a sea change in the war. Maybe this is the start of the end, where we really take it to them instead of waiting for the FALs to pop up as they will."

She intended her statement to soothe the others, but as she spoke, she felt a surge of pride. This entire operation was a tribute to what humanity could do. Four tasks forces, the height of human technology, represented a huge investment in time and resources. The fact that generations of scientists and engineers were even able to create the force and send it half a galaxy away was mind-boggling. And then there were the half a trillion people, working out their lives, paying their taxes to fund such a force. She felt honored to be taking part, whether in this particular battle or not.

And this was only 18% of the entire Navy. If the FALs knew what was good for them, they'd take their crystal asses and flee human space once and for all

****

Beth took a last sip of Coke, emptying the Number 6 dispenser. She'd meant to try and ration it out better, but six hours had tested her discipline and found it wanting.

The commander kept feeding them updates, and from all evidence, the battle was going well. There had been casualties, but that had to be expected in larger-scale battles. The FALs were on the run, however. Beth had expected them to jump out of the system, but if they wanted to stay and fight, it was their funeral.

By them not jumping out, though, Beth didn't see any quick victory in store. This was going to take awhile.

Should have held off, she told herself as she sucked on the tube one more time, trying to get every last molecule of Coke she could squeeze out of it. Thank goodness for Josh, though. Mercy's plane captain, AT1 Lena Lipscomb was such a stick-inthe-ass, always-by-the-rules suck-up that she'd never allow such a heinous breach of regulations.

"Yes, a Coke. So heinous!" Beth said with a laugh.

"Stand by for update," the commander passed.

Beth frowned. There was something different in his voice.

"What's up, do you think? Maybe we're getting sent forward?" Mercy asked hopefully.

"Not sure," Beth said. "Maybe—"

"Fox and Hotel, take up a Sierra Sphere around the *Victory.*
Full alert!" the commander passed.

Beth reacted immediately, giving the order, but her mind was whirling. What was going on? A Sierra Sphere was a closein, last line of defense posture. Beth checked her display as the *Tala* jumped to get into position. There was no threat that she could see. The ships started to change their relative position, but there was no sign of the enemy.

"What the fuck?" Mercy asked. "What's going on?"

"Steady," Capgun passed. "We'll find out soon enough."

But it wasn't soon enough, at least as far as Beth was concerned. It was seven long minutes of silence before the commander came back on the net. "The *Perseverance* has been lost." *What?*

"Crystal fighters, accompanied by what seems to have been a capital ship, jumped into their ROA. The remaining forces are trying to fight back."

"What kind of capital ship? How many FAL fighters?" Mixmaster asked.

"We . . . we don't know. The situation isn't clear," the commander said, for once, his calm voice showing signs of stress. "Until we know, we're in Condition Alpha, and I want you to be ready for anything. The admiral is recalling the forward elements now."

Beth was in shock. The *Perseverance* was the sister-ship to the *Victory* and the flagship of Task Force Iron Lance. And it was gone? The entire ship, just like that? That just couldn't be. One of the most powerful military platforms ever built, and it had been destroyed?

She had to force her mind back to a semblance of a degree of functionality as the *Tala* moved into position. If the *Perseverance* could be destroyed, then so could the *Victory*.

"Capgun, what . . . what the fuck's going on?" Mercy asked as the lack of further communications raised the stress levels. "Are they telling you anything more than what the skipper passed?"

There was no answer.

"Capgun?"

"Oh. What?" he finally asked.

"I asked if they're telling you any more than what the skipper told us about the *Perseverance*. I want to know what's going on."

"No. I'm in the dark like you," the acting flight leader said, his voice trailing off.

"Capgun. You OK?" Mercy asked, concerned.

He didn't sound right. Not that that was surprising. They'd all taken a gut shot, and the stress levels were skyrocketing. But he sounded different.

"Diane," he said. "She's on the *Perseverance*."

"Who's Diane?" Beth asked.

"My little cousin. She's an ensign on the *Perseverance*. *Was* on the *Percy*, I mean."

"Shit, Capgun. Sorry," Mercy said. "Were you close?"

"Very. I used to babysit for her and Danny, her brother."

Beth knew she couldn't let him stew. They might very well be facing the same threat, and he needed to be combat ready.

Time for some tough love.

"Snap out of it, Capgun. I'm sorry, but there will be time enough to grieve later. Right now, we've got two-thousand souls on the *Victory*, and we're part of their defense. OK?"

There was a long pause, then finally, "You're right. Later. Now, if those fucking FALs show a fucking crystal nose here, I'm going to shatter their asses."

Beth couldn't help herself. "That's redundant. 'Fucking Fucking Alien Lifeforms.'"

It was an old joke, but it worked.

"They deserve a second 'fucking.' F-FALs!" he shouted into the mic, sounding like his old self.

"F-FALs. I like it," Mercy chimed in.

The three Wasps slid into position, and with Hotel Flight, formed a protective sphere around the *Victory*. A very loose sphere with plenty of gaps, but along with two monitors and the other capital ships, it should be enough.

****

"We've got an unknown incursion into the sector," a nameless voice passed into the net, a palpable tension in his tone.

Not that the warning was needed. Alarms on every vessel were blaring. Something, and something big had just winked into the space some 500 kiloklicks from the *Victory*. Beth knew in her heart that it was a crystal capital ship, something that had been theorized but never yet seen.

Unless that's what hit the Percy, she told herself. *Or our forward forces at Tantalus 5.*

Reports from that fight, at least those disseminated to the pilots, were non-existent. Non-existent, but relevant to the extent if the forward assault elements could jump back to help defend the main body of the task force.

Beth half-expected to hear the order to start a retrograde out of the ROA, but she wasn't surprised when it wasn't given. The brass knew this kind of confrontation was inevitable, and the Navy of Humankind was not known for shirking a fight. And if they did cut and run, that could mean the loss of the *Stephens,* the *Silver Mountain,* and the Exemplar Wasps. No, she knew the admiral was going to slug it out right here. One crystal ship facing nine Navy men-of-war.

While waiting for orders, she zoomed in her display on the crystal ship. It was huge, but not much larger than the *Victory.* As she watched, the leading edge seemed to start to disintegrate, pieces of it falling off.

"What's going on with that thing?" Mercy asked.

The tiny particles that "fell" off started to orient, then form up in a mass heading towards the human ships. It all fell into place.

"It's not falling apart. Those are crystal fighters breaking off of it!" Beth said, an instant before the announcement was made over the task-force-wide net.

"Incoming crystal fighters," the voice passed calmly, then not-so calmly and with a breach of communications procedure, "Sixty-three . . . seventy . . . shit, the numbers keep growing!"

Orders were immediately downloaded, and the entire fleet—fighters, drones, and other capital ships—started to maneuver to provide a picket around the *Victory,* oriented to the oncoming horde of FAL fighters. Beth didn't like being controlled like a chess piece. She wanted to the freedom of choice. She was a pilot, after all, not a passenger. But she understood the need for interlocking fires to maximize their effectiveness, and that by ceding at least temporary control to the big combat AI on the *Victory* was the best—no, only—way to achieve that.

"Are the others coming back?" Mercy asked as they watched the approaching swarm.

"Don't rightly know, sista. If they're engaged . . ." she said, trailing off.

If they're engaged, it's just us.

Not just the Wasps, of course. Two of the destroyers were already firing, their big cannons putting out petajoules of energy. Within a few minutes, individual crystal fighters were winking out, but they were only drops in the bucket.

A moment later, the *Victory* herself fired two of the 40meter-long MX-100 Orion ship-killer missiles. Beth's attention was on the fighters, though. Those were her targets, and she ran though firing solutions after firing solutions as they approached, waiting for orders.

But the swarm of fighters didn't seem to be heading for the *Victory*, the logical target for them. Unless they were going to converge from a different direction, they were going to pass by the main body of the task force.

"Where the hell are they going?" Mercy asked.

"Just keep focused," Capgun said. "Be ready for anything."

The *Victory's* combat AI shifted the positioning of the forces slightly, forward facing the maximum power. The *Tala* slid into position, her own AI indicating that her torps had a 92% probability of a hit among the closest FALs. Yet the order to fire never came.

The *Tala* wasn't the only one. "I can splash one of them right now," Mercy passed on the flight net. "I've got a 94percent POS."

"Hold on," Capgun said again. "Wait for weapons free."

The DS *Xhosa* and *Wintergreen*, a frigate and a corvette, broke their place in the formation and started to advance to the most highly concentrated mass of crystal fighters. They were escorted by a dozen drones. Neither of the big ships was specifically designed to take the attack to smaller opponents like the enemy fighters. That was the Wasps' mission. But with only seven Wasps, the admiral obviously thought that the *Xhosa's* Acrix self-defense system would be equally as effective in the attack. With the *Wintergreen* and the drones, she represented a powerful punch.

Timelines were getting shorter as the forces closed. Eleven minutes after breaking out of the defensive shield, the *Xhosa* opened up with her MX-49 Hedgehog. Able to track thousands of targets at the same time, her AI continually arranged them with regards to their threat potential. Each volley of the Hedgehog consisted of 50 DD-303 meter-long, semi-autonomous, hyper-velocity missiles. The mass of crystal ships took notice. About a third turned toward the frigate while the rest continued to who-the-hell-knew-where. The *Wintergreen*, with her single massive hadron cannon, poured out petajoules of energy, sweeping the oncoming fighters.

The first volley of the 303's cut a swath through the crystal fighters. Beth gave a victory yell in her cockpit. There was still a shitload of crystals out there, and more were on their way, but the *Xhosa* had proven herself an effective platform.

The second volley didn't splash as many, and Beth frowned as she analyzed her display. It should have. The 303's were on target. The third volley was even worse, with only seven FALs getting splashed. Somehow, in an unbelievably short amount of time, the FALs had adjusted. Impossible, but she couldn't ignore what was on her display. Her thrill of victory of only minutes before turned to foreboding.

"We need to go help the *Xhosa*," she told Capgun.

"Wait one," he said, then came back only ten seconds later with, "That's a negative. Remain in your position."

Sixty-three crystal fighters closed in with the *Xhosa* and *Wintergreen*. Small blips appeared on Beth's display, leaving the FALs and heading toward the two capital ships. They didn't have the same reading as the crystal torpedoes previously used, but they had to be weapons.

The *Xhosa* and *Wintergreen* were recalled, but the two ships couldn't turn on a dime. Mass and momentum were harsh mistresses. The *Xhosa* switched her Hedgehog system back to defensive mode, and it started knocking out the new torpedoes, but Beth knew it was only a matter of time. There were just too many of them. As she watched, feeling impotent, the first of the torpedoes hit, then another. Beth wasn't tied into what was going in, so she didn't know how damaged the frigate was. She hoped the shields were holding up, a hope that was crushed when the *Xhosa* exploded, followed by the *Wintergreen* a minute later.

Beth stared at the screen in shock. This couldn't be happening. Two ships—two capital ships—had just been lost. Close to 700 sailors had been killed. Taken out by crystal fighters?

The *Victory's* main combat AI took over again, repositioning the task force to maximize their defensive posture. Beth wasn't in control as the *Tala* shifted its position.

More and more of the FALs were flaking off the big ship and heading towards the task force. But the enemy ship had a surprise coming. The two Orions were streaking at it with nuclear hellfire burning inside of them. Beth watched on her display as the two missiles reached the second wave of fighters, blasting through them to reach the main ship. But they didn't make it through. The crystal fighters, in turns that seemed to defy the laws of physics, swung around to match the shipkillers' course. But they didn't fire their beamers. They didn't fire their torpedoes. Instead, they seemed to close in and blanket the missiles.

"What the hell are they doing?" Mercy asked.

Beth didn't know, but she watched, her attention split between the Orions and what the AI was doing with her *Tala*. As the Orions, with their blanket of crystal fighters closed the distance to the big enemy ship, they started to swing wide.

They're pushing the Orions off-course, Beth realized.

She was gobsmacked. What she was observing would be impossible for current human technology to accomplish. She wasn't sure humanity would even try it. Defenses against antiship missiles were either to burn them with energy weapons or to blast them with kinetics. Humans didn't try to simply shove them off course.

But it was clear that was what was happening. The Orions' internal guidance systems were straining to bring the missiles back on target, but without effect. They were going to miss.

The proximity triggers detonated first one, then the other Orion at their closest approach to the oncoming crystal ship. A hundred or more fighters, the ones shoving the missiles aside, were atomized, but Beth couldn't tell if the explosions had any effect on the main ship.

She knew her flightmates were watching what happened, but no one spoke. It was a lot to take in.

The *Tala* reached her new position, and control reverted back to Beth. She still didn't have any specific orders, but she felt better.

The *Victory* had two more Orions in her launchers, but she didn't fire. Beth guessed that the admiral wanted to retain them until the distances were less. That would give the FAL fighters less time to react. But that was a wicked game of timing. Too early, and the Orions could miss again; too late, and the flagship could be taken out before it even fired.

But the *Victory* and the other capital ships had energy weapons, hedgehogs, and a host of other defenses. Sweeping vast tracks of space with energy weapons was not effective. Focused beams were. FAL fighters fell, but targeting individual fighters took time, and there seemed to be an unending supply of them.

Beth held back, an unwilling observer. She was a fighter pilot, and she wasn't released to fight.

"The commander is launching," Capgun passed on the flight net.

"The commander? He's grounded," Mercy said.

"I guess he just got un-grounded," Capgun said, not sounding too happy about it.

Beth realized the she wasn't surprised. She'd even expected it on a subconscious level, not only because it increased the Wasp force by 15%, but this was probably the last time Commander Tuominen would fly a Wasp, the last time he could prove himself. She doubted that the commodore nor admiral even knew that he was launching. And there he was, streaking out from the Victory and heading in their direction.

With the Xhosa and Wintergreen gone and the drones ineffective, the main swarm of fighters swept forward. Their target was clear by now. It was the *Chon Buri*, the massive supply ship.

The *Chon Buri* was mostly automated with only a small crew of thirty-seven, but it carried the massive amounts of food, equipment, and weapons needed to keep a task force operational far from the friendly confines of a home port. It wasn't a man-of-war, though, armed only with anti-boarding weapons and one torpedo tube. She didn't stand a chance. Beth kept waiting for the orders to be given for them to rush to help her, but her speakers remained silent. There wasn't much they could do, though, she knew. The crystal fighters would swarm the *Chon Buri* before any of the Wasps could reach her.

Beth watched in dread resignation as the FAL's closed in. The *Chon Buri* put up a fight, spitting out a dozen M-57s, but it was a foregone conclusion. She was a big ship, however, bigger than the *Victory*, and it took nine FAL torpedoes before she broke apart.

"Well, fuck," Mercy said over the flight net. "Why the *Chon Buri*, though?"

"It looks like the FALs are targeting by size," the commander answered. "They might have thought the *Chon Buri* was the main ship in our task force."

That sounded weird, but who knew? The FALs were an alien lifeform, and no one could expect them to match human thinking and logic. At the moment, however, Beth didn't care why the FALs did what they did, only that the Navy be able to stop them. And on that tack, things were not looking good.

****

Things were still looking bad thirty-minutes later. No more Navy ships had been lost, but the vast interlocking dance of FAL and humans as they maneuvered and counter-maneuvered did not show an advantage for the good guys. More FAL fighters had sloughed off the main ship as it slowly approached, and the task force was gradually being compressed, like anchovies hounded by dolphins off the coast of California. She didn't see an easy way out even with the rest of the Stingers shooting the gate back to them.

Her display chirped, and Beth looked to see other launches taking off from the *Victory*, these one depicted in olive green.

It took her a moment to remember what that meant.

The Marines? They're getting into this?

The Marine Corps of Humankind was mostly used for ground operations, but they were all trained in ship-to-ship take-downs, making the transit in their Moths, which were nothing more than bare-bones shuttles with a forced-entry attachment, a single small hadron cannon, and a modicum of shielding. A Moth was not a real fighter, and it wasn't something in which Beth would ever want to go into combat. From the looks of it, however, the Marines and their Moths were being thrust into battle against the FALs.

Thirty-two Moths were launched, but instead of pressing against the crystal fighters, they were . . .

Beth didn't need her AI to run a probability analysis. She could see that they were heading for the big crystal ship.

That can't be right. It would be suicide! This isn't some pirated passenger liner that needs to be retaken.

But it *was* right.

"Fox and Hotel Flights, break out and provide support to the Marines," the commander passed. "They need to reach the crystal ship, and we need to see that they do. Your positions have been uploaded, but we are weapons free. Take any action you deem necessary."

"Commander, the Marines?" Capgun asked. "What are they going to do? Force entry and take over the FAL bridge?"

"They're carrying NN-50s," the commander answered back. "They're going to get in close and emplace them on the target,
and if necessary, force entry after the detonation."

Holy shit!

The NN-50 "Asteroid Buster" was a tectonic nuke, designed to breach under-the-surface installations on asteroids, moons, or even planets. With minimal maneuverability and slow speed, it was usually fired from less than a hundred klicks—*klicks*, not even kiloklicks. This made it almost useless as an anti-ship weapon, but it would be effective if it could somehow hit the thing.

The admiral was using the Marine Moths as a booster stage to get the NN-50's within range. Technically feasible and probably in one of the operating manuals, but had it ever been used? Beth doubted it. And then the Marines were supposed to breach whatever part of the ship survived?

But if the FALs could take out the Orions, how could the Marines survive long enough to launch? This was a disaster waiting to happen.

She vowed to do her best to protect the Marines, but even with the commander joining them, there were only eight Wasps. That was only 24 torpedoes, their most effective weapon, and after those had been launched, they'd be down to their hadron cannons and rail guns.

We just have to make it work.

A stray thought hit her. Thirty-two Moths weren't much, but how many NN-50s did the *Victory* carry? She pulled up the T/E. If the data was up-to-date, the *Victory* had eight of them. The *Chon Buri*, which was no longer in existence, had another sixteen in her stores.

That meant that twenty-four of the Moths didn't even have one of the weapons aboard. Since they were ineffectual fighters, those Moths were simply there to draw fire. They were rushing to battle without a way to fight.

Crazy snake-eating grunts, she thought in admiration.

With the *Chon Buri* destroyed, the swarm of crystal fighters had already begun a wide loop back. Beth knew they weren't quitting the field of battle. If the commander was right, and the FALs were prioritizing their attack to the largest target, that meant the *Victory* would be next. Beth had to hope that the task force would be able to withstand the wave of FALs, and she hated not being part of the defense, but she understood the mission. With the big crystal ship still shitting out fighters, they had to cut that off. And if an attack on their mothership might cause the fighters to pull back to defend the behemoth, then all the better.

In typical military fashion, where service turf had to be protected, interoperability suffered, Beth couldn't talk to any of the Marines. The commander probably had comms with the Marine colonel, but she didn't. She switched to visuals on the nearest Moth to her. The distance was still too far, and the image wasn't clear. But inside that normal-looking shuttle would be 48 Marines in their combat armor, sitting and waiting, unable to take charge of their destiny.

The Moths and Wasps charged forward, closing the distance with the big crystal ship, while behind them, humans and FALs were clashing. Beth began to hope that the 40 vessels were too small, moving too relatively slow, to draw notice.

Wishful thinking.

"We've got company," Capgun passed as a group of 62 FAL fighters adjusted to an intercept course.

The FALs began to fire, the traces of their energy weapons showing pink on Beth's display. None of the Wasps were being targeted, only the Moths. Which was stupid. The Moths were not a threat and wouldn't be for another twenty minutes. Tactically speaking, the FALs should strip the

Marines of the Wasps, first, then pick the Moths off at their leisure.

But the Moths are bigger than we are, it dawned on her.

The big, bad FALs had screwed up by attacking the Chon Buri first instead of the *Victory*. And now they were ignoring the superior firepower of the Wasps to take on the Moths. While tactically stupid, it was strategically sound, Beth realized, even if the FALs lucked into it. But Beth intended to make them pay for ignoring the Wasps. She was continually running firing solutions and target prioritization, ready to unleash.

The Moth's shields were degrading, but they were still holding firm. The Wasps had to act, though, before the Marines started to get splashed.

"Hold your fire," the commander ordered. "I'm taking us off weapons free. The FALs don't seem to realize that we're the ones who can take them out, and I want to keep it that way for a little longer. I want a 75% POS before we fire the 57s. We can't afford to waste any."

"Rough on the Marines," Mercy said on the S2S.

Which was true. But the strategy was sound. There were 62 of the FALs engaging them, and if they were going to have any chance, each torpedo had to splash one of them before they resorted to their cannons.

"It won't be long, Mercy. I'm showing a 62-percent POS now."

"I know. I just want to finally splash one of the fuckers. I guess this is my time," Mercy said, her voice subdued.

Yes, Mercy. You'll get your first kill. Too bad we won't be around long enough to celebrate it.

And she knew it was true. Back in the main fight, the *Makepeace*, a corvette at the leading edge of the battle, had just taken heavy damage, even if she was still barely operational. The *Victory* was taking intense fire. As Beth looked up at her battle display, one of the unmanned monitors ceased to function, eliminating a significant chunk of the task force's interlocking defense.

Moving to engage the Marines were the 62 FALs, and if the eight Wasps somehow managed to keep them off of the Moths, the huge crystal capital ship loomed large. Beth felt a flicker of despair, which she angrily shoved back down, letting her warrior emerge. If she wasn't going to survive, she was going to make damned sure she took as many of the bastards out as she could.

She flipped to the flight net and said, "Yes, it *is* your fucking time, sista! Let's go kick some crystal ass! You, too, Capgun!"

"Satan's balls yeah!" Mercy shouted. "The sisterhood!"

"Sisterhood? Does that include me?" Capgun asked with a laugh.

"Better believe it, Capgun. You're a sista as far as I'm concerned!" Beth yelled into her mic.

"About fucking time you invited me," Capgun said. "I'm proud to be a sista!"

"Then let's get at them," Beth said, just as the first Marine Moth winked out.

"Weapons free," the commander passed over the command net. "Engage at will!"

Beth immediately launched all three torpedoes, one after the other. She didn't even bother to track them. They'd hit or not without her mentally urging them on. She switched to her P-13 and started pouring gigajoules out, first in a single spread pattern to get the FALs' attention, then focusing the beam to take out individual ships.

The crystal fighters finally took notice of the eight Wasps. The *Tala* was hit, her shield alarm screaming at Beth. She didn't care. She wasn't going to get out of this alive, so her full attention was in attack mode. Her target juked like a jackrabbit, but Beth kept the lock, blocking out the alarms.

"Yee-haw! I splashed the motherfucker!" Mercy shouted. "I got my kill!"

Beth didn't bother to check, but she keyed her mic and said, "Way to go, sista. Now get number two!"

The FALs fired off their torpedoes, most at the Marines, but at the Wasps as well. Beth ignored them as she poured power into her cannon, robbing it from her shields. To her surprise, her target disintegrated, sooner than she'd expected. She shook her head, then made sense of her alarms.

"Shit!" she said, juking the *Tala* hard to her right and below the elliptical, but the FAL torpedo was locked on her. She'd been so focused that she'd put herself into danger. Beth knew she wouldn't survive the battle, but she couldn't afford to go out after only one kill of her own. If the task force was going to have any chance, they couldn't let this turn into a battle of one-forone attrition.

She fired her cannon at the incoming torpedo, ready to hit G-Shot to put some space between them when the torpedo exploded less than 70 klicks from the *Tala*.

"Keep your head on swivels, Beth. I need you," the commander said on the S2S.

Beth checked her display. The commander had taken out the FAL torp. He had come to her rescue. She felt a wave of shame wash over her. There was too much going on for him to have to watch over her.

And "Beth?" He just called me "Beth."

She didn't know what that meant, and she didn't have time to consider it. She had to fight smarter.

Beth checked the combat display. Out of 21 torpedoes, 18 had splashed FALs. All three of hers had run true. Two of Mercy's had.

Twenty-one torps? Who didn't fire? she asked herself before checking her display. *The commander? Why didn't he launch?*

She didn't have time to figure out why he hadn't fired. Eighteen out of twenty-one was good, but not good enough. And the FAL torpedoes were taking their toll as well. Mixmaster was gone, and the Marines were getting hit hard. Nineteen of the thirty-two Moths had been taken out. As she watched, one more was splashed.

Beth didn't have time to figure out who that was. She pulled out her silver cross from underneath the collar of her flight suit and kissed it in memory of the Marines, then let it fall to her chest, outside of her flight suit. Highly non-reg, but what the hell? She'd felt better with it in the open.

She latched onto a torpedo targeting one of the remaining Moths. The Marines understood the threat, and they were engaging the torps with their hadron cannons, but the little guns had nowhere near the power of the Wasps'. It was a futile endeavor. But Beth pushed her P-13, upping the power and dangerously raising her temperatures. She started pumping out fireturds, but her temps still rose. She could become DIS because of overheating just as easily as being hit by an enemy torp. But she held on while her display redlined, refusing to let the Marines down.

At the last second, her onslaught broke through, and the torpedo lost its lock. The Moth was able to juke and get out of its path.

"Fox Flight, on me," Commander Tuominen passed just before the lead elements of both forces reached each other. "Keep them off of me."

"Sir? What about the Marines?" Capgun asked.

"Change of plans. Their attack is broken. On me now," he ordered, breaking in front of the FAL approach. "Hotel, stay with the Marines. Do what you can." *What the hell? Abandon the Marines?*

Beth's mind churned with confusion. There were six Moths left, and she couldn't just leave them with the three remaining Hotel Flight Wasps for protection.

"On me, now!" the commander ordered one more time, the proverbial Golden Tribe tone of command almost jumping out of her speakers.

Navy discipline kicked in, and Beth inputted the orders into the *Tala*. The four Wasps broke off, each one guiding on the commander.

"What are we doing? Mercy asked. "Are we running?"

"No! I mean, I don't think so," Beth answered.

But she didn't know. Could the commander be trying to save his own ass? She thought she knew him better than that, but maybe not . . .

"What are we going to do?" Mercy asked.

"We're going to obey orders," Beth snapped. "That's what we're going to do.

Beth didn't think she could live with herself if they ran from the battle. Maybe the commander had some knowledge that had to be gotten back to Navy HQ, but she was just a low-level pilot, nothing more. And she was leaving behind her fellow pilots.

She checked the battle display again. Two more ships, the *Blue Marlin* and the *Brindisi* had been lost. Hundreds of crystal fighters had been splashed, but there were just too many of them hounding the remaining ships. And more kept flaking off the main ship, which seemed noticeably smaller than it had been when it appeared in their sector of space. It was as if the fighters were part of the main ship, sent off to fight the humans.

Beth now knew how the *Perseverance* and Task Force Iron Lance had been defeated, and it looked like the same thing was in store for them. Out at Tanatalus Five, the *Stephens*, the *Silver Mountain,* along with the Exemplars, were probably lost as well, and it looked as if they'd been set up all the while by the FALs. The commander and Fox Flight might survive the battle, but to what end? Just to report back what happened? The Admiralty, back at Navy HQ, would be monitoring the battle and they already knew the task force was getting slaughtered.

"Shields off. Full power to stealth scramblers," the commander ordered.

So, we're going to try and sneak away? Beth wondered.

But orders were orders. She made the switch. She was resigned to the disgrace of abandoning the Marines and Hotel. Even if they made it back, they'd most likely face a courtmartial.

Without their shields, getting hit now would be lethal. That might be preferable.

"Tuna just made ace," Capgun said.

Beth switched back to Hotel. Petty Officer Second Class Areesha "Tuna" Lymon, the junior pilot in the squadron, had splashed three FALs with her torpedoes. While Fox Flight was running, she'd gotten another with her P-13, and she'd just splashed one more with her rail gun.

"Good for her," Mercy said without a trace of jealousy.

Tuna, the last of the surviving Hotel Flight Wasps, was trying to protect the last two Marine Moths, but it was obvious that her time was up. No fewer than eight crystal torpedoes where incoming while the enemy energy cannons were degrading her shields.

"Kick some ass, Tuna!" Beth shouted over the command net.

"Comms blanket," Commander Tuominen ordered.

Beth felt a surge of anger at him. A blanket was not a blackout, but it meant no unnecessary communications that could break their stealth mode. She hoped that Tuna heard her, to let her know she wasn't alone . . . even if she was.

And then it was over. Tuna managed to evade the first torp, but the second one got her. Beth took a dozen deep breaths, regaining control. Officer or not, she was going to give the commander a piece of her mind when they got back.

"We're not running away, Beth! Look at our track!" Mercy shouted excitedly.

Lost in her thoughts, Beth hadn't been following their route. She pulled it up on her display, and what Mercy had said became clear. There was only one reasonable destination, and that was the crystal ship itself. They were looping around to come at it from the side.

Beth felt a surge of excitement, of relief. The commander was not running, after all.

"Listen up," Commander Tuominen passed on the line-ofsight laser comms. "We're in stealth mode for a reason. The FALs seem preoccupied with size as a threat, so we've got to remain small. They will detect us at some point, however. I'm sure of that. When that happens, initiate the clone projector. Give them something to think about. And then keep the FALs off of me. Understand?"

"Yes, sir," the other three pilots said.

Beth knew now why the commander hadn't fired his three M-57s. He'd foreseen what would happen, and he wanted them for his own torpedo run. But would they be enough? That was a huge ship out there, and the M-57's were not designed for anything so massive.

Maybe they can damage it so it will pull back, she told herself unconvincingly. If the enemy had countered the Orions, then they shouldn't have too much trouble with the much smaller, much slower, M-57.

Beth, Capgun, and Mercy formed a triangle around and slightly ahead of the skipper. It wasn't a great defensive formation, but it was the best they could do with only their three Wasps. Together, Fox Flight closed the distance with the big crystal ship, all the time watching for any sign that they'd been detected.

It happened too soon. They were too far out, but four fighters turned to orient themselves to the flight. Beth didn't think they could detect the Wasps, but rather their bow wave as the human fighters hurtled through space.

"Initiate G-Shot," the commander ordered. "On my count." *G-Shot?*

Beth did a quick calculation. Even with max acceleration, it would take almost 20 minutes to be within reasonable torpedo range, and the human body couldn't take G-Shot for that long.

"It's too far out, sir," she said on the comms.

"It's our only choice, Beth," the commander answered back.

"You told me, back on Earth, that you've never G-Shotted before."

"Then it's high time I did, don't you think?"

"That's not what I mean. It's unbelievably hard to endure."

"You did it. Twice."

"Not for this long," Beth said. "Just wait until we're closer."

"We can't. I need to build up my speed. All of you, on my count. Five . . . four . . . three . . . two . . . one . . . initiate!"

"Mother of Mercy," Beth whispered, kissing her cross as she initiated G-Shot. The familiar, agonizing fire flowed through her veins as the *Tala* jumped forward, matching the commander's acceleration.

She grunted in pain. This was her third time hitting G-Shot, and it was worse this time. She'd been told that residual cell damage made each successive G-Shot more painful, but she had underestimated by just how much. She needed a mantra to clear her mind, but she couldn't think of one until, in her torment, an image popped into her head. She was, ten years old and in a white, lace-trimmed dress, kneeling at the front of their village church for her first communion.

> *Hail Mary, full of grace.*
> *Our Lord is with thee.*
> *Blessed art thou among women,*
> *and blessed is the fruit of thy womb,*
> *Jesus.*
> *Holy Mary, Mother of God,*
> *pray for us sinners, now and at*
> *the hour of our death.*
>
> *Hail Mary, full of grace.*
> *Our Lord is with thee . . .*

It worked. The pain was still there, but compartmentalized. She could still function. She could still fight.

It took the four crystal fighters a couple of minutes to react by reorienting themselves. The FALs had to realize that something was out there, something approaching them.

They weren't stupid. Two of the FAL fighters fired their energy cannons, sweeping in a wide pattern. The *Tala's* alarms screamed, interrupting Beth's prayer. With the FALs' beams spread out, this was just a brief kiss.

Without her shields up, however, even a kiss could be lethal. The ship held together, but her fingers tingled, and she thanked Jean-Luc and all the rest of the R&D team for her neck-cracker. She knew she wouldn't have survived even that brief hit without it.

"Initiate cloning," the commander ordered, acting immediately. "Then drop stealth mode and shift full power back to your shields."

Beth immediately reacted. That energy beam touch had broken through her G-Shot pain better than her prayer had.

The four ships would now be apparent to the FALs, but appear as eighty. In theory. There was still no evidence that it confused the FALs. But it was their only possible course of action at the moment to get the commander in close enough for his torpedoes to have a chance.

It took the oncoming FALs several minutes before they reacted, spreading out and launching four torpedoes apiece, then firing more focussed energy beams. Maybe the clone projector was spoofing them after all.

"Hold your fire," the commander ordered, his voice showing no strain from the G-Shot. "Don't give out your real positions until we have to."

Typical GT, Beth thought. *They can even take G-Shot better than us norms.*

He was right about holding their fire, though. Beth itched to strike out, but until R&D could develop clones that could fire real weapons, then the four of them needed to remain hidden among the spoof Wasps for as long as possible.

"Here comes the cavalry," Mercy passed.

Beth shifted her display. The rest of the initial 62 FALs were shifting to orient on them. Only one Moth was still intact, so the supposed 80 Wasps that suddenly appeared had to be posing a bigger threat.

Get out of there, Beth wished on the Moth before turning her attention to the FALs.

"Beth," Mercy passed on the S2S, her voice straining with the effects of G-Shot. "I just wanted to say . . . I mean, it's been great having you as a sister. To be accepted into your family . .
."

"You are my sister, Mercy. Not just through you marrying Rocky. You've always been the sister-of-my-heart. Sistas forever."

"If I don't, you know . . . let Rocky know I love him."

"He knows, sista. He knows," Beth said.

She wasn't going to bullshit Mercy, to tell her that either of them was going to talk to her brother again. This was going to be it. Even if the commander could somehow get through to the enemy ship, there were still hundreds of crystal fighters who wouldn't be too happy with them.

Her alarms went off again. She'd been hit, and her shields dropped to 52%, but they were holding. The *Tala* was still combat-effective.

Keep it together, girl, she told her Wasp, giving the front of her cockpit a pat.

But the clone spoofs seemed to be working. FAL energy beams were spread out, the torpedoes tracking nothing real. Beth started running scenarios. For several of them, the odds of getting the commander into range were approaching, if not probable, at least possible. Those scenarios all depended on keeping the crystals from locking on their positions.

As usual, an enemy rarely cooperates. One of the enemy torpedoes locked onto Capgun.

"What are you orders, sir?" Capgun asked, his voice straining under G-Shot induced stress.

There was a long moment, and Beth knew what was going on in the commander's mind. The best bet for the other three Wasps was for Capgun to simply ride it out. Capgun could take evasive action. He could take the incoming torp under beamer fire. But the moment he did, the lead four FALs would make the connection between real and fake. As the rest of the FALs started engaging the Wasps, they'd watch to see who took evasive action, then focus on that target.

That would be suicide, though, to just wait until the torpedo reached him. The commander had that horrible decision that made Beth glad she wasn't in charge. Was improving his chances of getting a good firing solution on the FAL ship worth the life of Capgun? They were all on a suicide mission, but he had to fire his torps.

Beth knew what the commander would say, and she knew Capgun would accept those orders.

But he surprised her.

"Continue on course," he passed, which was what she expected. "At two-hundred kiloklicks, engage the torpedo. Take it out," he continued, which she didn't expect. "Make them react."

"Roger that, sir," Capgun passed back, his voice full of enthusiasm. "I'll give them something to focus on."

Beth checked the time. Capgun had almost six minutes to run quiet, six more minutes that the commander could use to get closer to the crystal ship. She ran the figures. Six more minutes would put them at the outside range of effectiveness. Fifteen would be better.

"Capgun," Beth passed on the S2S.

"It's OK, Beth. I'm about done-in here. This fucking G-Shot . . . at least I'll be finished with it."

Beth didn't know what to say. Since joining the Stingers, she'd become close to him. Her own two big brothers had left New Cebu to become Off-Planet Workers when she was only five, and Capgun had filled that roll in her life. The thought of going on without him hurt deeply, even if her own time left was limited. His excuse was pretty lame, but it was easier just to accept it.

"Yeah, I know what you mean. This is my third G-Shot, and it sucks big time."

"Beth, get the commander through. Make it all worthwhile," Capgun said, suddenly serious.

"I will. I promise."

"Hey, Mercy's trying to cut in," he said with forced cheerfulness.

"OK, talk to her," Beth said, choking back a sob.

She cut the connection and sat in her cockpit, feeling alone. On her display, the slow-motion dance of humans and FALs continued to play out. One way or the other, the end game would be revealed in fewer than twenty minutes.

She kept running scenarios, ranking them by order of probability of success. None were great, but there was no backing down now.

As the clock ticked on, she kept glancing at Capgun's icon, wondering when he was going to make his move. The enemy torpedo was quickly approaching.

She was expecting it, but it almost surprised her when Capgun cut his G-Shot and fired, yelling, "Here I come, assholes!"

At the close distance, his beamer tightly focused, it took only seconds to knock the torpedo off course. Even with his GShot cut, he wouldn't be 100%, but he wouldn't get any worse as he turned his Wasp into the oncoming FALs that were trying to cut them off. Within a minute, the mass of crystal fighters was shifting to meet him and his 20 ghost clones. Not a portion of the enemy. *All* of them.

Beth tore her eyes off of Capgun's trace to look at her scenarios. The probabilities were all climbing. They weren't great by any means, but much better.

"Hold your course," the commander told Mercy and her with no hint of G-Shot stress.

That was one of the most difficult-to-obey orders Beth had ever received. She watched Capgun, her friend, charge 62 FAL fighters, cannon a'blazing. Within moments, the FALs started to converge on the *Lovely Rita*, ignoring the cloned images. Energy beams reached out to him, bathing him in Tango rays. But he was giving as good as he got. He poured gigajoule after gigajoule out of his cannon, splashing the first of the nearest four FAL fighters, then the second.

The loud, discordant chords of "Armadillo Punch," Capgun's favorite song, filled Beth's cockpit. Beth always hated the song and told Capgun so whenever she could, but now, she sang along as he took the third FAL under fire.

I hate the way you play me, babe,
But I'll still worship you the ground you walk on.
I'm a stinkin' armadillo, lost in the—

The music cut off, and Capgun was gone, a FAL torpedo finding its way to the *Lovely Rita*.

Beth gulped, then whispered, ". . . lost in the cage of your presence."

"Steady," the commander said. "We've still got our mission."

Beth stared at Capgun's icon for a moment, now red on her display. As if remembering that there were still humans there, the flight of crystal fighters started to orient on the three Wasps, again, angling to cut them off. But Capgun had given the human pilots a little breathing room—not much, but some.

Would it be enough?

In-depth thinking was becoming more and more difficult, but she was able to monitor the *Tala's* AI as it kept running calculations. Beam weapons reached out to her, some lingering on the *Tala*, degrading her shields further. The POS, which had been improving, started to fall again. No matter how she changed the course of action, it did not look good. The commander would have to launch from too far out, giving the target too much time to react.

The commander had the same calculations, but he wasn't going to accept that.

"I'm going to push to MaxG," he passed to Mercy and Beth.
"Do your best to keep them off of me."

"Sir, you can't take it," Beth immediately protested. "And your Wasp won't allow it."

G-Shot enabled a pilot to withstand about 80Gs, far above the 40Gs a Wasp's internal compensators allowed them. MaxG was the maximum acceleration a Wasp could do, which was far beyond the ability of the human body to endure, and was only used in some remotely-piloted circumstances. A Wasp had a failsafe that wouldn't allow the fighter to even approach MaxG if there was a pilot aboard.

"I've got an override, Beth. And it's the only way. You can see the POSs."

Beth hadn't even allowed for MaxG. She quickly ran the scenario. It gave a 38% POS, which was still poor, but better than any of the others.

"But that assumes you can survive it, sir."

"I only have to survive it long enough. And accelerate to a high enough speed."

It hit her right then. The commander had never intended to launch his torpedoes. He'd known his only chance to significantly damage the big crystal ship was to make his Wasp the weapon. He was going to ram the big ship. But he didn't understand that G-Shot wouldn't save him. He'd die long before the Wasp would reach the enemy ship.

"Sir, you can't—"

"I have to," he said, interrupting her. "You and Mercy, you just keep them off of me."

"Aye-aye, sir," Mercy said, but the commander had already cut the connection.

A moment later, the *Kalma* leaped ahead like a racehorse down the stretch, leaving Mercy and Beth behind.

"Think he'll make it?" Mercy asked.

"No," Beth said. And that was the truth. "But he has to try, and we have to help him." That was also the truth.

She fed in another scenario, noted the POS, then bounced it to Mercy.

"Really?" Mercy said a few moments later.

"You see the POS," Beth said.

There was a sigh, then, "Then let's do it."

Beth kissed her cross, then together, the two Wasps, followed by their 40 clone images, started to swing around to face the pursuing crystal ships. They had reacted to Capgun, so maybe they'd react to the two of them as well, giving the commander a better chance.

Beth swung around her cannon and started engaging the enemy. That was giving up her position, so in a moment of defiance, she turned off the clone projector. She wanted the FALs to see her, to know that Petty Officer Second Class Floribeth Salinas O'Shea Dalisay, Navy of Humankind, was coming after them.

The FALs started converging on the two Wasps. It was working. Whether it would make a difference or not was another matter, but this was the best that Beth and Mercy could do.

To her surprise, she almost immediately splashed one of the FAL fighters. She wondered for a moment if these were not front-line fighters, something akin to the Marine Moths. That gave her a moment of hope before she was hit and had to juke out of the beam. These fighters might not be as robust, but they still packed a powerful punch.

She shifted to the next target and started pouring fire onto it. Combined with incoming fire, her shields struggling to protect her, and her own outgoing fire, her temps started to rise.

She initiated her fireturds, but didn't cut down on her joules.

"Look at the ship," Mercy told her.

She glanced back, and as the commander approached, there looked to be a flurry of activity as more FAL fighters detached themselves from the main body of the ship. These seemed to swing to orient to the approaching commander.

"I think those new FAL fighters are the ship's close in defense system," Mercy passed.

Beth thought Mercy was right. The new fighters, which moments before had looked to be part of the ship's integral structure, started to pull away from it and head towards Commander Tuominen, who was quickly closing the distance.

"Beth," the commander passed, his voice barely a whisper.

"Sir?" she answered as she kept up her own fire.

"I just wanted to tell you. I'm so glad I grabbed you out of Hamdami Brothers. You've been special, and not just to the . . ." he said, pausing as if to gather himself. MaxG had to be killing him. "To the Stingers. To me. I've lived a privileged life, while you . . ."

Yes, I know I come from a meager background.

"You've made the best of your situation. I . . ." he said before trailing off.

Beth wondered if he was still alive, and she asked. "Sir? Are you there?"

Her alarms were blaring, and her shields degrading, but she felt a sense of loss.

"Still . . . here. Not for long. You showed me what it . . . means to fight on. I was going to quit. But you . . . prove yourself . . ."

"I made you stay on? To prove yourself?" she shouted into her mic.

There was no answer. But the *Kalma* was still on target. He'd have put it on autopilot, letting the Wasp fly herself. He might be dead. He might be unconscious.

But her speaker crackled one more time, and a weak voice said, "I wonder what might have been between us in other circum—"

And she knew that was it.

She tried to force more power into her P-13 by pure force of will. She and Mercy could try and pull back now. They'd given the commander the window he'd needed, at least from this group of FALs. There were still the ones leaving the ship, and as she watched, something else started spitting out and reaching for the *Kalma*. Something kinetic.

But to what end? The *Victory* was damaged, but still alive. For how long, though? Three other ships were still fighting, but there had to be five or six-hundred FAL fighters still in the fight as well. If she and Mercy managed to break away, they would still be outnumbered, unable to use the gate which Navy HQ had already blown. They were stuck out here until a rescue, a rescue that wouldn't be coming.

"You with me sista?" Beth asked.

"With you, sista!"

The two pilots swept in closer to each other, cannons blazing.

"That's five!" Mercy shouted as she splashed another of the FALs. "Satan's balls, I'm a fucking ace."

Beth hadn't been counting, and despite the dire situation, she was impressed. Five kills in a single mission?

"Damn, girl! You're killing it!" she told her friend.

"I want to get one more before the end," Mercy said.

"Then let's do it," Beth said, firing off her railgun along with her hadron beamer. No use holding anything back, and she could get lucky. There were certainly enough targets out there for her.

Her alarm switched to short, blaring blasts. Her shields were at 5% and dropping.

"No! Not yet! One more first!" she shouted in anger, targeting another crystal ship.

She risked a glance at the commander's icon, surprised at how fast it had closed the distance. Less than a minute now, and the *Kalma* would reach the ship. Her heart skipped a beat. Now she wanted to live long enough to see him hit the ship instead of splashing one more FAL.

As for the crystal ship, it was now pulling back, off of the only course it had been on since its arrival. It was too late, though.

"Get it, get it, get it!" she shouted into her mic.

"Look at him go," Mercy said. "Do you think . . .?"

"Yeah, I think—"

And the *Kalma* was hit by one of the crystal kinetic rounds.

Beth could see it come apart, just ten seconds from the ship.

"No!" she screamed, oblivious that her shields were at two percent and ready to fail.

But physics is physics, no matter with humans or aliens. Just because the Wasp had come apart didn't mean it was stopped dead in space. The mass of debris, to include three armed torpedoes, slammed into the crystal ship at close to .80C. Beth's mind couldn't calculate the numbers, but the force had to be tremendous. A flash blinded her display until the *Tala* could compensate, and when it came back into focus, most of the ship was gone, vaporized. Beth had been able to witness it before the fighters took her out.

"Mercy, he did it," she said. "And we saw it happen. I hope Commodore LaRue did, too."

If the commodore was still alive. The *Victory* had taken some hits. With what were probably her last thoughts, Beth wished that the admiral was still alive, that she had seen how wrong she was about Commander Tuominen.

Except, it wasn't her last thought as she instinctively targeted another FAL and fired, splashing it within seconds.

"Beth, what's going on?" Mercy asked.

What was going on was that there was no incoming fire. No beamer fire. There were torpedoes, but they seemed locked on their previous course, now heading harmlessly off into space.

She looked at the crystal fighters, and they looked . . . uncontrolled?

It hit her in a rush.

"The FALs! They're Dead in Space!" she shouted.

Chapter 22

"Another three hours and I'll have her up and running," Josh said, wiping his hand on the rag hanging off his tool harness.

"OK, let me know," Beth said, surveying the hangar deck.

It was depressingly empty. Where it had once been full of fighters, there were only the *Tala*, the *Louhi*, and the still unassigned spare, just pulled out of storage.

Fifteen other Wasps had survived the battle: four of the Exemplars and eleven Stingers, but they were still on the other side of the destroyed gate, waiting for a new one to be emplaced. That wouldn't be happening for quite some time, however. The admiralty was being cautious, fearing another trap. The *Victory's* scouts had survived, but they were out in the black providing a screen for the remnants of the task force that had so proudly sallied forth to face the enemy.

Task Force Iron Shield had won the battle, as the admiral had pointed out over the ship's internal media to the surviving crew. The crystals had been completely defeated. Not a single one was left alive. The science teams aboard the *Victory* were still arguing the specifics, but the basic facts were clear. The FAL fighters were components of the larger, "hive-ship," as it was being called. They were the soldier and worker ants, breaking off to do whatever they were supposed to be doing.

Beth thought that was a bad analogy, however. Soldier ants didn't immediately die when the anthill was destroyed. She thought the fighters were more akin to nanos that were controlled by a central AI. If the AI was taken out, the nanos lost their instructions and became so many tiny pieces of junk.

When the commander—or at least the *Kalma*—slammed into the hive-ship, whatever control system it had was destroyed, and that cut the command link with all the fighters, leaving them rudderless. That exposed a huge vulnerability in the crystal forces. The FAL fighters might be able to function far beyond the physical presence of a hive-ship, but the thinking now was that there would have to be a hive-ship out there somewhere. Think-tanks were already hard at work trying to determine how to locate and destroy them, rendering the fighters ineffective.

The task force would not be alone for long. Teams were on their way to examine the huge numbers of fighters that were now inert. More vital was the husk of the hive-ship.

Beth looked over to the other occupant of the hangar. The last Moth was now in Bravo Hangar what with their own Charlie Hangar damaged in the battle. After the commander took out the bulk of the ship, the Marines had landed on what was left and breached it. What had been Capgun's facetious comment about Marines taking over the bridge had turned out to be the case. Whether it really was a bridge or not remained to be determined, but after a bloody fight, the Marines had cleared the ship of living crystals. Twenty-four Marines, along with over a hundred sailors, were now on the hulk, keeping it secure.

Mercy entered the hangar, spotted Beth, and beckoned her over.

"I just talked to him," Mercy said, as Beth reached her.

"I thought the admiral said we're in a comms blackout."

Mercy shrugged and said, "It's who you know, sista. I didn't tell him much, just that we're both fine. There're rumors that something's up, but I left it at that."

Mercy had probably done enough by just contacting Rocky to land her in the brig for 30 years, but Beth didn't care. Neither of them was the commander. Neither was Capgun, nor even the Marines. But they'd been in the thick of the fight, and Beth didn't think the brass would want to make an issue of it.

"What now?" Mercy asked as the two looked out over the hangar.

"Now? We've got a key to the FALs' weakness. We let the science-types figure out what we can do to exploit that. We let the engineers create the weapons to do it. Then, it comes down to us, the fighters, to take the fight to the bastards, to kick their crystal asses out of the spiral arm and make them afraid to raise their ugly heads here again. That's what we do, Mercy," Beth said with vigor as emotions threatened to overtake her.

"It's always up to us, isn't it?" Mercy said.

"Us. The Marines. Warriors. That's what we do. That's what we've always done so the rest can live their lives."

"What about the Stingers?" Mercy asked. "Do you believe the commodore?"

"I don't know, sista."

Commodore LaRue had been adamant that the Stingers were not done. They would be brought back with new pilots and new Wasps. "In honor" of Commander Tuominen, she had hypocritically insisted.

But it wasn't up to her. That would be far above her paygrade.

And Beth wasn't sure she wanted the Stingers to come back. They had been the brainchild of Commander Tuominen, his baby. He created them, trained them, and commanded them in battle before he died, and it didn't seem right that there would be another commander. Beth could fly with any squadron and do her duty, but maybe the Stingers should be retired.

The commander wouldn't be forgotten. His family, the ones who tried to keep him out of the Navy, would make sure of that. His fame, and he would be a god-hero once the public knew what happened, would be exploited by them, used to advance their political and economic goals. It would be great if the Stingers could be placed into memory, the one place where he wasn't a GT, but just their commanding officer.

"I'm going to miss him, Mercy," Beth said.

"Capgun? Yeah, me too."

Yes, Capgun. The commander. Wingnut. All of them.

The two stood side-by-side quietly, looking out over the hangar. Finally, Mercy broke the silence with a soft, "You know,

I was jealous of you." "I
know," Beth answered.

"I'm so sorry about that. I just wanted a kill. Hell, I
wanted to be an ace, like you. Now? I'm not so sure it's that
important."

Beth was about to agree. She barely thought of being an
ace anymore. The loss of life in the last battle had hit her
hard. All her friends. All her compatriots. She'd give up
being an ace, she'd give up her Order of Honor, just to get
them back again. But just as she opened her mouth,
something clicked, and she said, "But it *is* important."

"What?" Mercy asked, turning to look at her, surprised.

"No, not the designation. That's just ego-fluff. One kill,
five kills, a hundred kills, 'ace' is just a label. The kill itself is
the important thing. You saw how many FALs hit us, right?
From that, I get the feeling that we humans are outnumbered.
That means we pilots have to rack up the kills. Tuna got in
five. Capgun got seven. The commander? Six hundred?
We're going to need each of us to kill as many as possible
before they splash us.

"So, it is important if humanity is going to survive this war.
We all have to rack up as many kills as we possibly can."

Mercy digested that for a moment, then said, "I guess
when you put it like that. But I was thinking more of the
honor."

"I know you were," Beth said. "And right now, I couldn't
give a rat's ass about that. I just want to kill more of them."

Mercy put her arm around Beth's shoulder and pulled her
close, saying, "We will, Beth. We will."

Beth tilted her head to lay it on Mercy's shoulder. After a
long minute, she said, "You know, I've been jealous of you,
too?"

"What? What the fuck do I have that you could be jealous
of?"

"Love. You found your soulmate."

"Because of you, sista. I envied your family, and I'm
grateful that I'm part of it now. You don't know how grateful.

And don't worry. You'll find someone, too," Mercy told her.

"I hope so."

There was another pause, then Mercy asked, "Was there really anything between you and the . . . you know? I mean, there were whispers."

Beth had been wondering about that ever since the command master chief had accused her of being the commander's pet. Was there really anything between them, or had she been reading into things that didn't exist?

"No," she said, almost convincing herself. "Just mutual respect. Anything else was in Orinoco's fantasyland."

"Yeah, that's what I thought."

If there had been a spark of potential, it didn't matter now. It was better not to dwell on something that probably didn't exist.

Down on the hangar deck, Josh pulled his head out of the *Tala's* nose compartment, spotted them, and gave Beth a thumbs up.

"That's my lover now," Beth said with a laugh. "Whenever I can get her away from Josh."

"He is a jealous one, isn't he? Look at him, stroking the *Tala's* skin like a lover. He'd probably fu—"

"Mercy!" Beth said in mock shock, pushing her friend away and cutting her off. "That's gross."

"Don't knock it until you try it," Mercy said, their mood significantly lightened. "So, are we going to stand here forever?"

"Satans' balls, Mercy," Beth said with a laugh. "We haven't had real food in how long? The galley's back in operation, so let's go get some chow."

"Good idea, sista. I'm starving."

Beth linked her elbow through Mercy's, and together, they walked out of the hangar, leaving Josh and Lipscomb as the two plane captains worked to get the *Tala* and the *Louhi* back to a combat ready status.

There was still a war going on, after all.

Thank you for reading *Ace*. I hope you enjoyed the book, and I welcome a review on Amazon, Goodreads, or any other outlet.

If you would like updates on new books releases, news, or special offers, please consider signing up for my mailing list. Your email will not be sold, rented, or in any other way disseminated. If you are interested, please sign up at the link below:

http://eepurl.com/bnFSHH

OTHER BOOKS BY JONATHAN BRAZEE

The Navy of Humankind: Wasp Squadron
Fire Ant
Crystals
Ace

The United Federation Marine Corps
Recruit
Sergeant
Lieutenant
Captain
Major
Lieutenant Colonel
Colonel
Commandant

Rebel
(Set in the UFMC universe.)

Behind Enemy Lines
(A UFMC Prequel)

The Accidental War (A Ryck Lysander Short Story Published in
BOB's Bar: Tales from the Multiverse)

The United Federation Marine Corps' Lysander Twins
Legacy Marines
Esther's Story: Recon Marine
Noah's Story: Marine Tanker
Esther's Story: Special Duty
Blood United

Coda

Women of the United Federation Marine Corps
Gladiator
Sniper
Corpsman

High Value Target (A Gracie Medicine Crow Short Story)
BOLO Mission (A Gracie Medicine Crow Short Story)
Weaponized Math (A Gracie Medicine Crow Novelette,
Published in *The Expanding Universe 3. Nebula Award Finalist*)

The United Federation Marine Corps' Grub Wars
Alliance
The Price of Honor
Division of Power

GHOST MARINES
Integration
Unification
Fusion

The Return of the Marines Trilogy
The Few
The Proud
The Marines

The Al Anbar Chronicles: First Marine Expeditionary Force--Iraq
Prisoner of Fallujah
Combat Corpsman
Sniper

Werewolf of Marines
Werewolf of Marines: Semper Lycanus
Werewolf of Marines: Patria Lycanus
Werewolf of Marines: Pax Lycanus

Soldier

Animal Soldier: Hannibal

To the Shores of Tripoli

Wererat

Darwin's Quest: The Search for the Ultimate Survivor

Venus: A Paleolithic Short Story

Secession

Duty

Semper Fidelis

Checkmate (Published in The Expanding Universe 4)

<u>Non-Fiction</u>

Exercise for a Longer Life

The Effects of Environmental Activism on the Yellowfin Tuna
Industry

<u>Author Website</u>

http://www.jonathanbrazee.com

<u>Twitter</u>

https://twitter.com/jonathanbrazee